PLAY IT IN REVERSE

VICTORIA ANGELIQUE

VICTORIA ANGELIQUE

TRIGGER WARNINGS

This book contains topics including murder, rituals, death, harm to animals, anxiety, drug use, alcohol, and sex. Please be advised.

"True courage is in facing danger when you are afraid..."

"She is protected by the Power of Good, and that is greater than the Power of Evil."

- L. Frank Baum, The Wonderful Wizard of Oz

DEDICATION

For the patients I couldn't save.

ONE
ADDISON

NOVEMBER 27, 2024

REDLANDS, MAINE

Only five minutes ago, Addison had been sending impatient glances at the clock that hung in the nurses' station. Now she felt the patient's ribs snap beneath her stacked hands.

Four minutes ago, she had been tidying up his room, making him presentable for the oncoming shift. Now sweat beaded on her forehead as she began a second round of compressions.

Where the hell was the crash cart? Over the hospital intercom, a melodic voice repeated, "Code blue, ICU fourteen," for what seemed like an eternity, yet no one arrived to assist her.

Two minutes ago, Addison's patient had gripped her arm with unexpected strength. His fingers pressed deep into her forearm. The nub of his severed index finger, now healed over, threatened to bruise her skin. Watching his cracked lips move, Addison leaned in closer.

"Darkside must die." He struggled to speak, his grip—what was left of it—tightening around her wrist. "My stuff, you have to keep it safe. Promise me . . . don't let them get to it." The patient began mumbling. "I am Oz . . . great . . . terrible . . ."

When his hold on her relaxed, his heart stopped. A green flat line sang a sinister song as it ran across the monitor. Addison's fingers pressed against the patient's neck, his wrist, his groin in search of a pulse, but it was absent.

Addison replayed his words in her mind while her body reflexively began compressions.

"One, two, three, four . . ." she counted aloud. Saline flushes and alcohol wipes catapulted from her scrub pockets onto the floor and into the crevices of the bed.

The wheels of the cherry-red crash cart squeaked down the hall, one of them wobbling like an old shopping cart. A male nurse with winter-white hair and a gait just as unsteady as the crash cart entered the room and began attaching defibrillator pads to the patient's chest. Addison studied the unfamiliar man as she squeezed the Ambu bag to deliver air to his lungs. Respiratory had yet to arrive. Their department had been just as understaffed and overworked.

"*Analyzing rhythm,*" the robotic voice of the defibrillator echoed as the flat line continued on its fatal path. "*No shock advised.*"

"Is anyone else coming?" Addison inquired through

labored breaths as she resumed compressions. The man shrugged and began clumsily struggling with the medication drawer.

"Can we switch?" Addison begged. "I don't know if I can keep this up much longer." She desperately needed to shake out her arms.

"Sorry, shoulder injury," the nurse replied, his eyes never meeting hers. "You're doing great, though." He finally gained access to the medications, then fumbled to assemble a syringe of epinephrine. Whether it was a result of age or indifference, it took him three attempts to screw the syringe into the Luer lock of the patient's intravenous line and administer the first dose.

"He's in here for sepsis; can we give him sodium bicarb soon?" Addison shouted. "He's probably acidotic."

The nurse shrugged again.

"We need some help in here!" Her voice cracked as she screamed toward the open glass door until her throat was raw. "Where the hell is respiratory? Why isn't there a doctor in here?" Both questions rhetorical.

Addison felt her eyes narrow in a fiery gaze and her lips tighten in determination. She began the next round of compressions and respirations, trying madly to maintain quality until she couldn't anymore. Her heart churned with desperation. This would be the sixth code blue she had been a part of in the past two weeks, and she knew in her bones how it was going to end. How could it not? Time was slipping away, and still no doctor in sight.

"Come on, please come back," Addison grunted, thrusting her body weight deeper into each compression, her black French bob shaking violently with each movement. Tears pooled in her eyes. "Somebody help us," she screamed.

Moments later, her hands dropped away. Checking the wall clock, Addison called the time of death: 7:42. Only then did an emergency room doctor finally arrive, staying just long enough to confirm the patient was deceased and sign any necessary paperwork.

Addison's senses fought to recalibrate as she returned to the nurses' station, her body still trembling. The oncoming night shift nurse loudly slurped the final bit of iced coffee from her cup, which she had been nursing instead of helping with the code. Addison begrudgingly sat beside her and gave her report on the patient in ICU 13, an intubated and sedated eighty-year-old female. Ice rattled as the nurse shook her cup. When Addison began to discuss ICU 14, the nurse flapped her hand in an effort to stop her, unable to speak as she chewed on an ice cube that was somehow too large for her mouth.

She swallowed. "That's not my patient, not my problem."

Addison's heart pounded, but she knew if she said anything she would burst into tears, so she held her tongue. She gathered supplies before returning to her patient's room to perform postmortem care and bag his body. No one else was going to do it. Certainly no one would do it with the dignity he deserved. While some nurses had the privilege of giving their patients their first bath, Addison had too often had the privilege of giving her patients their final bath. To her, it was an honor.

As she stood at his bedside, her eyes traveling over his pale, drawn face, she recalled how he'd been found unconscious the day before at the emergency room entrance without any identification. He had been quickly admitted as a John Doe and transferred to the ICU for septic shock, which had developed from an unhealed gunshot wound to his abdomen. Most of her shift he had been too weak to talk, but he always mouthed *Thank you* even after the smallest task. He was a kind man. Or at least that's what she chose to believe.

With a gentle swipe, Addison closed his eyelids, then squeezed his hand.

"I don't know how much more of this I can take," she said, tears falling from her eyes. "I'm sorry I couldn't save you." She composed herself and began cleaning the body, removing any medical devices that were still attached. Her pathetic male counterpart had taken the crash cart back to central supply for restocking and had yet to return. She doubted he would.

As she worked, her patient's last words began flitting through her mind. *My stuff, you have to keep it safe.* But safe from whom? Placing her balled-up washcloth on the patient's chest, Addison knelt down and searched the side table for any personal items. Shoved deep in the back corner was an opaque patient belongings bag. It would be easy to sneak the bag into her backpack, which hung from the back of a chair in the nurses' station just a few feet away. The hospital camera system had been down for months, and the other nurses were busy assessing their patients and administering medications. It was wrong, she knew it, but the devilish side of her consciousness kept digging at her. She couldn't save his life, but she could honor his dying request. Besides, she reasoned, half the time no one picked up the belongings of a John Doe. They likely would end up in the trash or collect dust on a shelf in the security office. Without another thought, she ran the bag over to her backpack and tucked it inside.

"Let's get this over with," the male nurse from before announced, startling Addison as she finished zipping up her backpack. He slipped back into the deceased patient's room. She pushed down the urge to scream at him. To punch him in the face. Put *him* in the body bag. How could someone be so insensitive?

"I'm sorry, I didn't get your name," she fished. Maybe she could report him. "I'm Addison. I don't think we've ever worked together before."

"Jack," he said flatly.

Together they finished maneuvering the patient into the body bag and onto the stainless-steel morgue trolley. Addison strained to see Jack's badge—all she needed was a last name—but it was turned around. She figured he must be a traveler or a registry nurse, though he could be one of the government-appointed nurses the hospital had been using. Short-staffed would be an understatement.

Addison had been one of the few staff nurses left at Jefferson Memorial Hospital until that morning, when she'd joyfully put in her notice. Though she wasn't sure what her next job would be, she was beginning to think it ought to be anything other than nursing. Frugal by nature, with the privilege of living in a paid-off house, she'd been able to save enough money to live on comfortably for well over a year. A tempting option.

Together she and Jack wheeled the patient into the elevator and down to the morgue. It was a short ride. Quiet. Yet the animosity was palpable.

A brief struggle to get the trolley out of the elevator caused Jack's badge to flip. *Michael Larson.* The image was of a much younger man with dark hair.

"The badge machine was broken," he said defensively, flipping the badge back over. "This one's temporary. It belonged to someone who recently quit."

Addison searched his face and body for the lie, but his expression was resolute. Considering the way the hospital had been operating of late, it wouldn't surprise her if they'd repurposed an old badge. Especially with the current turnover rate. Besides, without a badge, he wouldn't be able to get into the units or supply closets.

"Look, it doesn't make a difference to me if you believe me or not." His words were sharp.

Neither of them said anything more as they slid the body into the cold locker exposing a putrid smell Addison could never get used to. As soon as the door shut, Jack vanished down the hallway.

"Good riddance," she murmured.

It was after 9:30 p.m. when Addison pulled into her driveway, defeated. She sat in the car for a moment, squeezing the tension from her left shoulder and arms, then burst out into a slimy, visceral cry. Snot dripped onto her lips, tears streamed down her cheeks, and she gulped for breath.

TWO
HANNAH

BERKELEY, CALIFORNIA

"LET'S DO SOME LSD," Hannah suggested, even though she knew Carrie wouldn't. Hannah loved that girl, but she was such a square. If they hadn't been best friends since kindergarten, there was no way they would have become friends in high school. Though they'd both started out as dorks, their trajectories were at odds. Both were bullied—which had brought them together in camaraderie—but for different reasons.

Hannah's dad had left when she was a baby, which somehow made her an outsider. Carrie wore thick glasses and had silver front teeth. Hannah never did understand why kids made fun of them, though. They were cool. Carrie looked like a pirate—a force to be reckoned with.

In middle school when they'd "found themselves," they discovered they were on opposite sides of the spectrum. Carrie had become head cheerleader, always wearing miniskirts and minidresses. Contact lenses supplanted the glasses, and beautiful, straight, white teeth replaced the silver ones. Her bleached-blonde hair was always styled to perfection, like Farrah Fawcett or any other supermodel plastered on the walls of every teenage boy's bedroom. She aspired to go to UC Berkeley, which happened to be right down the street from their neighborhood, and her grades reflected that. She was going to be a psychologist. Hannah believed the real reason Carrie wanted to go there was because of her boyfriend, Rodney, who had just started his freshman year on a full-ride scholarship. They were the typical cheerleader-and-quarterback couple, both equally smart and beautiful.

Hannah, however, was neither.

Hannah's mom didn't allow makeup in the house, claiming that it thwarted modesty, always sprinkling in a New Testament quote for fortification. Because of this, Hannah couldn't cover up her acne; Carrie's tan foundation would look ridiculous on her pasty-white skin. As if that weren't bad enough, her mom couldn't afford to take her to a salon. Unfortunately, the last time Hannah had trusted her mom to cut her hair at home, she'd ended up looking like a boy. Instead of taking that risk again, Hannah had let her hair continue to grow until it was down to her waist, secured in a Dutch braid.

Since the bands Hannah liked were "devil's music," according to her mom, the best she could do to express herself was wear all-black clothing. Hannah's jaw nearly hit the floor when her mom surprised her with a pair of slip-on Vans skate shoes one Christmas. Her mother believed that if she was going to give in to her rebellious nature, she should at least focus on becoming a professional skateboarder and make a career out of it. To Hannah's mom, as risky as such a profession might be, it was better than listening to AC/DC and doing drugs.

"Come on, Carrie, just once," Hannah pleaded. "I know a guy at Berkeley. We can pick it up while we visit Rodney in the dorms."

"You can do it," Carrie replied. "I have an important exam tomorrow."

"You're no fun," Hannah teased her as they walked onto the university campus.

"Not everyone needs to be high to have fun," Carrie said in her perfect voice. Hannah rolled her eyes. *Not everyone can get through the day without being depressed,* she thought to herself.

"It's my escape."

The girls entered Rodney's dorm, which was conveniently located right across the hall from Hannah's drug dealer, Paul. If she were just a little bit older, she would date him, but she doubted he'd want to date her. He played guitar and was majoring in music theory. Tall, trim, and charming. He was the kind of guy who knew and impressed everyone. The kind of guy who could get any girl he wanted, a notion Hannah couldn't compete with.

"Let's meet up later," Carrie whispered as Rodney lured her toward his bedroom. They'd be in there for hours. The thought of sitting in the cluttered living room, watching football with the four sweaty cavemen who were Rodney's roommates, repulsed Hannah—a feeling that was undoubtedly mutual, had they even noticed she was there, so she left.

Hannah could hear Pink Floyd playing, though muffled, behind Paul's door. Listening to music with him was an amazing experience, not just because he was handsome and smelled good—like musk and vanilla—but because he was a self-proclaimed audiophile. Apparently the drug money was good, because he owned the best audio equipment on the market, or at least that's what he'd told Hannah. He didn't just have the biggest speakers you'd ever seen; he also had a Sherwood receiver with integrated power amplifier and a Thorens TD 125 turntable. Music sounded majestic at his place, an experience arguably better than watching the band play live.

"Hannah, come on in," he said calmly, holding the door open.

Walking inside was like being transported onto a tour bus or backstage. Records lined the walls, and music permeated the air. Recently played instruments rested against furniture. Empty beer bottles were scattered across the floor, and ashtrays with partially smoked cigarettes spilled over onto stacks of magazines. Hannah sat on the edge of the couch, tucking her hands beneath her legs and taking in the smell of freshly smoked marijuana that lingered in the air.

"What can I help you with today?" Paul asked, standing over her with authority, his hands resting just inside the pockets of his tight brown trousers. He rarely sat down.

"LSD," Hannah said, her voice soft and feeble.

"LSD," he smirked, revealing a dimple. "Are you sure?"

"Yes, I'm sure."

"You've never done LSD, Hannah. Do you know what to expect?"

"I know it's a hallucinogen."

"You really should do it with someone experienced for your first time. Do you have someone you can do it with?"

Her pulse quickened. She thought about lying, afraid he wouldn't sell it to her if she was honest. "No, I tried to convince my friend Carrie, but she didn't want to."

"Do you have a curfew?"

"No—well, I do, just not tonight. My mom thinks I'm staying over at Carrie's."

"I see." He nodded. "And where is Carrie?"

"Having sex with her boyfriend."

Paul walked over to the couch and sat next to Hannah. "I'll do it with you." The corners of his eyes creased into his chiseled face, both brutality and kindness in every lineament.

Her stomach fluttered. His knee was just inches from hers. A magnetic energy pulled at her. "Are you sure? You don't have to do that," she said out of courtesy. In reality, Paul was the only person in the world she wanted to do LSD with. Maybe it would help him overlook her flaws.

"I want to." He retrieved a small lockbox from the coffee table from among a pile of *Playboy* and *Hustler* magazines. It was where he kept most of the drugs he sold. "I want to make sure you're safe."

"Right now?" Hannah asked, her palms beginning to sweat.

"Right now," he said suavely, pulling out a small square of paper that resembled a lottery scratcher. It was white with rows of little rainbows. Taking a small pair of nail scissors, he trimmed off two squares.

"How much do I owe you?" Hannah asked.

"Don't worry about it," he said, tapping the bottom of her chin. She opened her mouth, and with a sly smile on his face, he placed a square on her tongue, where it began to dissolve. Hannah imagined he was thinking, *Good girl.* Then he slipped the other square onto his own tongue.

"What do you want to listen to?" he asked as he approached his wall of expensive music equipment, which took the place of a television. The Pink Floyd record had ended, and while he waited for an answer, he slipped it back into its sleeve.

"Do you have any Black Sabbath?"

A glass cabinet housed rows of albums, all arranged alphabetically. His fingers danced across the albums' spines until he reached the one he had been searching for. The album was black with Black Sabbath written in purple lettering. It was the *Master of Reality* album. Hannah knew this because it had her favorite Black Sabbath song on it, "Sweet Leaf," which also happened to be the first track.

Slipping a Pall Mall cigarette between his lips, Paul cradled a flame with his hand, then swayed to the music, exhaling a puff of smoke. His body was loose and liberated. Hannah sat on the couch like she was Velcroed to it. It wasn't until twenty minutes later that she began to loosen up. A rush of euphoria released her from her apprehension. Paul placed the cigarette in her mouth. She took a long drag as she swayed her body to the rhythm, first matching the music, then matching him. The cigarette became moist from both their lips. Soon, even the walls were swaying to the music.

After a quick trip to the kitchen, Paul returned and handed Hannah a beer, which, after only a few gulps, she clumsily spilled on her shirt. She tried to clean it up, but the fabric was soaked. Paul disappeared into his bedroom for a moment.

"Here." He tossed her a wrinkled Pink Floyd shirt to put on. Hannah gripped the shirt, waiting for him to turn around so she could change, but his gaze never faltered. She peeled the soiled shirt from her slender figure, standing exposed in her ugly tan bra. A bra that no one was ever supposed to see. His scent filled her nose as she pulled the new shirt over her head. The fabric draped loosely over her pale skin.

———

"Do you like plays?" Paul asked. They were now outside, walking arm in arm, their gait sluggish, toward Hearst Greek Theatre. Colors splashed vibrantly before

Hannah's eyes. Bushes inhaled and exhaled as they shuffled past. Somewhere along the way, the day had slipped away, and darkness enveloped the college campus.

It was that night that Hannah experienced what true happiness felt like for the first time. Warm honey swam through her body. Sweet. Comforting. Surreal. A euphoria that blotted out any trace of depression. If she were home, she'd probably flush her antidepressant pills down the toilet. Surely she wouldn't need them anymore, or so she thought.

"They're wonderful," she lied. Though she'd never been to a play, the thought of seeing one excited her.

They entered the theater on stage right, looking out into a vast bowl of empty seats. Behind them, a colonnade gave the theater an appearance that was true to its name.

"These are my friends," Paul said, introducing Hannah to a group of college students. There was Jane, a naturally beautiful woman with long blonde hair. Yessenia, a peaceable overweight Hispanic woman. Franklin, whose dark, deep-set eyes hinted at his Italian background. There were a few others that greeted her reverently.

A record player was set up in the center of the stage, with speakers on either side. White and black candles were arranged to form a circle. Jane led the women in a chant as they lit the candles with grace.

Hannah's eyes grew heavy. Her head spun as she drifted away into darkness for brief moments of time. Was this the effect of the LSD, or had she been slipped something else? This feeling was not novel. It felt exactly like the time she'd had a panic attack so severe the doctors had pumped her full of quaaludes to calm her.

A needle scratched against vinyl, catching her ear. Then she heard a familiar, yet unusual, sound.

"Is that 'Sweet Leaf'?" she slurred.

"Good job," Paul said, catching her as she stumbled across the stage.

"Sweet Leaf" was playing in reverse. If only her mom were there to hear it. If she thought Black Sabbath sounded demonic forward, it was unimaginable what she would think of it backward.

A verse graveled, "The price of darkness."

Everyone chanted "The price of darkness" in unison as they closed in on Hannah like synchronized evil swimmers. Their bodies pulsed in and out. Hannah continued to lean against Paul, but she was getting weaker. She battled the urge to close her eyes. Paul hoisted her into his arms, not to rescue her but to place her in the center of the candle circle.

"He lives," the song sang.

"He lives," the group chanted.

The flames blossomed to implausible heights, casting a fiery glow on each circling face, rendering them ghoulish.

"My divine," Jane declared as her dress flapped in the cold October wind, "we call on you for council. We've brought a young woman like you asked. Guide us to grant your wish."

It could have been the drugs, but Hannah swore the

flames flickered immediately after Jane spoke. Whoever, or whatever, she was calling on was listening.

Yessenia raised her arms to the sky, like she was preparing to conduct an orchestra. Someone pulled out an Ouija board and set it up on the stage just outside the circle. Everything glowed orange as the record continued to play in reverse.

Jane dipped the wick of a long black candle into the flame of another, then blew it out. A trail of smoke snaked upward. She pressed her fingers against the blackened wick, then stepped back into the circle. Jane's body looked giant to Hannah as she stood over her, growing taller and taller, as if Hannah were Alice in Wonderland after she'd downed the *Drink Me* potion. Jane traced a triangle onto Hannah's forehead with ash, then knelt behind her. Her slim fingers wove into Hannah's hair. Squeezing a thick chunk, Jane tugged Hannah's head backward. Frigid air grazed her exposed neck.

"I want to thank you for your sacrifice." Jane's whisper tickled Hannah's ear. Her voice was different now. More sinister, like caramelized sugar left to burn.

Hannah struggled to fight herself free, but her fists were heavy. Like a vignette, blackness squeezed at her periphery.

"What?" she was able to mutter.

"Your blood sacrifice," Jane seethed.

The rest of the group had their hands stacked on the planchette of the Ouija board, asking for guidance. Something caused it to move. It began to slide all over the alphabet.

Jane retrieved a dagger from beneath her dress and pressed it against Hannah's throat. The pressure of the blade caused her to choke.

"I think your blood is going to taste exceptionally good," Jane said. Hannah flinched, causing the blade to nick her throat. Blood soaked the edge of the blade. Jane salivated. This was it—Hannah's life was ending, and for the first time in a long time, she didn't want it to.

"Wait." She recognized Paul's voice even with her eyes closed.

"What is it?" Jane asked, not relaxing her pressure.

"We've received a message." His footsteps drew closer. "She is chosen."

Jane gasped, dropping the dagger to the stage. Hannah's vision went black.

THREE
ADDISON

Warm yellow light caressed the front of Addison's red-shingled house, its Craftsman-style charm still in evidence despite the chipping paint and a roof in desperate need of repair. Ivory trim encased rain-dappled windows.

The sidewalk was wet and cracked between patches of snow, a mirror reflecting back the glow of the streetlights. Addison unloaded her silver Toyota 4Runner, hoisting her worn JanSport backpack over one shoulder. It was first car she had purchased as a nurse and the only brand-new car she had ever owned. Snow crunched beneath her feet, then the porch creaked. Her house was old, both inside and out.

Her keys clanked into a green Pyrex bowl that sat just inside the front door. Lamps flickered to life, revealing a shag-carpeted living room adorned with plants. Plants hung from the ceiling by macrame ropes and rested in windowsills. Pothos vines spilled down dusty bookshelves ridden with half-read classics and never-read contemporaries.

A linoleum hallway led to the kitchen, where Addison dumped her stuff. She unpacked the leftovers she had intended to eat for lunch. As she yanked her Jefferson Memorial sweater loose, her patient's belongings bag tumbled onto the heat-worn dining table. It was wrinkled and opaque, yet radiating with mystery.

A shower, pajamas, and the rest of last night's blunt preceded her return to the microwave, where she reheated her chicken teriyaki. She had been five years old when her father brought home the now-yellowed Panasonic microwave. The days of eating out every night had come to an end along with her mother's career, a segue into a life of frugality. Even with all of its stains, splatters, and burn marks, Addison intended to use it until it died. She did this with everything else she owned, a value her father had managed to instill in her during the short time he was around.

The same original birch-plywood cabinets from her childhood clothed the kitchen walls. The teal Formica countertops and harvest-gold stove had been installed during the house's construction, though only two burners worked now. The house was a seventies time capsule that Addison had been living alone in since she was seventeen.

Every night her mother would disappear to the Rusty Tavern, a local dive, where she could always be found sitting at the bar, her bare legs crisscrossed, nursing a Scotch on the rocks with a twist. Sometimes she would return later at night with a random man. Sometimes she wouldn't return until the morning. But the last time, ten years ago, she'd never returned at all.

For Addison, it was much easier to grieve the loss of her mom. When she was seven, her father had abandoned them. It was quick. Explosive. There was no time to say goodbye. No time to process. Her mom, however, had slipped away slowly and steadily. Picked apart one night at a time by alcohol and famished men until she too was gone. That night, for the first time, Addison smoked the rest of the lipstick-smeared joint her mother had left behind. Each crackling inhale offered solace, each exhale a whisper that it was going to be okay.

Addison's fork scraped against the bottom of the orange-stained Tupperware as she shoveled rice into her mouth. Her knees were folded into her chest at the head of the dining table. She slid her phone closer, ready to begin catching up on all the texts and notifications she had missed.

VERONICA

Addy, you ok? Did you get stuck at work late again? Call me ASAHP (as soon as humanly possible) xo

NORAH

How do you know when a nurse is having a bad day?

MRS. WELLS

Hi honey, I wanted to invite you to Thanksgiving tomorrow at my house, don't bring anything, I would love to have you.

CASABLANCA NOTIFICATIONS

You have received 3 new messages from Chris

CASABLANCA NOTIFICATIONS

You have received 2 new messages from Tye

Addison texted Veronica back first:

Yeah I'm good, rough day at work, but I'm home now. Call you in a minute.

Then her friend Norah:

By being the friend of a nurse who had a bad day?

Last, Mrs. Wells, her neighbor across the street:

Hi Mrs. Wells, thank you for the invite, I'll see you tomorrow.

Addison swiped to the incoming text:

NORAH

No, she won't stop needling people :D

But I have been told I was eerily intuitive

ADDISON

Good joke but bad timing. And by who? Professor Hanson?

NORAH

Aww, today was supposed to be a good day, putting in your notice and stuff

Hey, Prof. Hanson was an intelligent woman

ADDISON

Putting in my notice was the only good part of the day, but sadly my patient died at the end of my shift

Professor Hanson was crazy, you were the only one in our nursing cohort that liked her and that's just because you two are equally as demented lol. Only a demented person would buy someone else a gift on their own birthday.

Norah had been born on Christmas Day, but, like the Hallmark Channel, she liked to celebrate it in July. As a firm believer in equity, she held that the summer babies shouldn't get to hoard the summers. Every year Norah threw a massive barbecue pool party where she watched each of her friends open a gift she'd handpicked and elegantly wrapped in newspaper and yarn. That year she had gifted Addison hard plastic cat knuckles with sharp pointed ears that hung from a key chain ring—one of the many benefits of hooking up with a tech guy who owned a 3D printer. (Norah had also scored printed coasters, boat parts, and a custom rack for her Nespresso pods.) As a result of peer pressure, Addison promptly attached the cat to her keys.

NORAH

I'm sorry about your patient Addison. Try not to be too hard on yourself. You were the toughest girl back when we were in nursing school and still are the toughest ICU nurse I know. I'm not sure how you have stuck it out this long at that hospital.

And, I'm by far the best Psych nurse you know ;)

ADDISON

Yes you are, and quite the diagnostician. In the five years we've been friends, you have managed to diagnose me with almost everything in the DSM-5 handbook

NORAH

Come on! That's not true, you only have GAD, separation anxiety disorder, social anxiety, dependent personality disorder . . .

ADDISON

Oh is that all?

NORAH

:)

ADDISON

You coming to Thanksgiving tomorrow?

NORAH

At your neighbors'?

ADDISON

Yeah

NORAH

I'll probably come grab a bite

Addison FaceTimed Veronica before opening the messages on her dating app, Casablanca—the app of "Chance Encounters," "Where the Unexpected Becomes Extraordinary." It was rule number one in their best friend handbook: *Thou shall not open messages from men alone.* Admittedly, a rule that was frequently broken. Veronica's freshly washed face filled the phone screen, catching the nearby glow of candlelight. Skin care was her religion, her routine intricate. Addison's routine, on the other hand, consisted of washing her face with whatever soap was available—a cardinal sin.

"Okay, I'm going to open the messages from Chris first," Addison announced.

"Has he asked you to be his girlfriend yet? It's been like a year since you've started talking, right?"

"Not quite, but it feels like it. It's been about six months. And I doubt he'll make it exclusive anytime soon," Addison replied, disquieted by her own sad inflection. "Everything is so easy when we're together, but I don't want to have to tell him what to do; he should be the one to take initiative."

"I still think you should just ask him yourself. Are you scared he'll say no?" Veronica tried to understand as she adjusted the pins in her onyx hair, which would later be released into voluminous wavelets resting at her clavicle. Her micro bangs would be curled to a level of perfection that would make Bettie Page proud.

"I'm not scared." Addison hesitated. "I just think the guy should be the one to make the first move. Call me old fashioned."

"Addy, babe, we've known each other since elementary school. I was the one that held you when your dad left, shaved your hair into a Mohawk during your punk-rock phase, the one you lived with for two years until you were ready to go back home after your mom. Need I say more? You might be able to fool your other friends, but not me. I know what's really going on."

"Oh really, and what is that?"

"You're scared of rejection," Veronica began. "You're afraid that if you're the first one to say *I love you* or to make it exclusive, he'll leave or say no."

Addison's eyes defiantly drifted from the screen.

"You know I'm right."

"No comment."

"You're going to have to face it at some point, babe." A beat. "Or, well, Norah's a psych nurse—maybe she could give you some medication."

Addison laughed. "Norah would just give me the nurse's dose of Ativan and call it a day."

Veronica laughed nervously. "Oh my gosh, Addy, you guys scare me sometimes."

Addison swiped to the dating app.

CHRIS

Hey Addy the Baddy

CHRIS

What you up to tonight?

CHRIS

Lemme know if you want me to come
over, would love to hang

"Addy the Baddy," Veronica teased. "Don't tell me you have a nickname for him too."

Addison broke her silence. "Chris the Kiss."

Veronica cackled. "That's not even good."

"That's it, now I'm not going to tell you what Tye said," Addison threatened.

"You wouldn't dare."

Veronica's retort was met with a sly laugh.

TYE

I've really enjoyed getting to know you
this past week. It's refreshing to meet
someone who is on the same page as I
am, wanting to get married and start a
family. With my 32nd birthday right
around the corner, I don't have much
time to waste, and every second I spend
talking to you never feels wasted—

Veronica stopped Addison as she was reading the message. "Okay, first of all, a little cheesy."

"Cheesy, but also kind of sweet," Addison admitted.

Veronica agreed. "And good for him for speaking what's on his mind. Okay, then what?"

TYE

Let me know what your schedule is like
this week, I would love to plan a date
for us.

"I don't think you've told me about this one yet," Veronica said. "He sounds pretty serious already."

"Well, we just started talking like a little over a week ago, maybe. He owns his own tech start-up business, which I guess he has already done one other time and sold for a lot of money. He has a border collie named Brutus—"

"Of course," Veronica interrupted, suggesting that Addison was interested in him primarily because of the dog. Something she had been guilty of in the past.

"His mom and sister are both nurses too, and he also loves eighties and nineties sitcoms."

"Which one is his favorite?" Veronica challenged.

"*Seinfeld.*"

"Okay, it's in our top three." Veronica nodded in approval. "Well, it definitely sounds like you guys have a lot in common," she admitted. "But the real question is, how cute is he?"

"Supercute. He has a kind of smoldering look to him. Dark hair and dark eyes." Addison sent over a photo.

"Wow, I never thought the day would come when Addy the Baddy would date a guy that wasn't blonde." Veronica smirked. "Oh, but he is so cute," she added once she received the photo. "He kind of looks like Jughead's dad, but kinder, if that makes sense."

"Yes! Total Skeet Ulrich vibes. I know, it's weird, that's not usually who I'd go for, but we really connected. We even like the same music—"

"Wait." Veronica stopped her. "Favorite Nirvana song?"

"'Heart-Shaped Box,'" Addison replied.

Veronica's brows scrunched, and her gaze drifted.

"Stop trying to figure him out based on his favorite Nirvana song. Life doesn't work like that," Addison said. They laughed and agreed that while it wasn't the best Nirvana song, it was a great contender.

"I'll just text Chris later, depending on how I feel," Addison said. "But how does this sound for Tye? *I have enjoyed getting to know you as well and would love for you to plan a date. I am free on Friday if you want to get together.*"

Message sent, with Veronica's approval.

"If things don't work out, you can give him my number." Veronica winked.

"Very funny." Addison grinned. "What's happening with your dating life anyways?"

"Nothing at all. It's actually really depressing." Veronica sighed. "Can you believe I haven't been with anyone since Carlos?"

"Ah, yes, Carlos the bouncer." Addison recalled the three-year relationship Veronica and Carlos had back when she was a burlesque dancer at Club 41.

"Carlos the cheater," Veronica corrected. After discovering his infidelity with two of the other burlesque dancers at the same club, Veronica had left Carlos and the profession entirely.

"I still don't get why you force me to get on Casablanca but you refuse to use dating apps."

"Because I want to meet someone naturally so we

have a cute story to tell at our wedding," Veronica said with hearts in her eyes.

"You think I don't want to meet someone naturally?" Addison protested.

"No, that's not what I meant by that. It's just that you would *actually* have to leave the house to meet someone naturally, and you are more of a homebody, that's all. Before we hang up, what happened at work? You said you had a rough shift?"

"Yeah, another really bad code blue." Addison sighed.

"Oh no, I'm sorry, babe."

"It's okay, thank you. It just kills me that I couldn't save him." Addison's breath caught in her throat. "We are so short staffed that I feel like even the patients that could have been saved ended up dying. I did everything I could, and it still wasn't enough. Literally the worst hospital in Maine." Addison rested her chin on hand. "On top of that, the oncoming nurse just sat in the nurses' station drinking her coffee."

"Wow, that's horrible," Veronica sympathized. "But don't let things that are out of your control make you question your ability to save someone. You are an amazing nurse and you've saved tons of lives over the years, unless you were making all of those stories up to look good. It's unfortunate that your hospital has gotten this bad, but as of today, you never have to go back."

"Praise be," Addison said, evoking a giggle from Veronica—a nod to another one of their favorite shows.

"On another note," Veronica continued, "how are people like that even allowed to work there?"

"You'd be surprised who they'll hire when they're desperate and want to save money." Addison shook her head. "Do you want to hear something weird?"

"Always."

"Before my patient coded, he grabbed me and said something that didn't totally make sense."

"What do you mean? What did he say?"

"Something like 'Darkside must die.'"

"That is creepy AF." Veronica's nose scrunched with distaste.

Addison told her about the incompetent nurse. Her barely-there blunt sizzled as she took a long, final hit. "The patient already had a low chance of survival, but I feel like this guy made sure he didn't. I know that sounds crazy, but I just have this gut feeling that something wasn't right."

"I am honestly shocked that hospital is even open. You absolutely need to report him, Addy."

Addison assured Veronica she would.

"All right, babe, I have to let you go; I have a client early in the morning. This super-rich lady wants to hire me to plan a safari gala—don't ask. Text me tomorrow."

FOUR
ADDISON

The patient belongings bag sat on the oak dining table, slouched and wrinkled. Addison tugged it closer. She checked the window blinds, confirming they were shut before releasing the drawstrings. Though she was simply abiding by her patient's wishes, somehow it still felt wrong.

The smell of sweat and dirt wafted from the bag as she pulled out a black T-shirt, a pair of white socks with blackened soles, and faded jeans. At the bottom were a hardcover book and a generic black unlabeled cassette tape. Addison quickly flipped through the vintage copy of *The Wonderful Wizard of Oz*. It was likely a first edition. Yellowed pages were filled with markings and annotations, meaningless without context.

As she stuffed the musty clothes back into the bag, a small golden key fell onto the table. She scraped it across the surface and into her hand.

"All right, Mr. Doe, what does this key go to?" she asked aloud.

Remembering her father's old tape deck, she bolted to the living room to find out what was on the cassette. It took her a couple of minutes to get the tape player to work. White noise blasted through the speakers, causing her to jump at first. She adjusted the volume.

"Number nine, number nine, number nine, number nine," the recording repeated with an ominous piano melody playing in the background.

It was oddly familiar. After three minutes of the same two words repeating, a piano began to play, accompanied by indistinct chatter. Then those words again, "Number nine." To quote Veronica, it was creepy AF. And uncomfortably reminiscent.

Jolted by the sound of her phone ringing, she smashed the stop button on the tape deck.

"Hey, you scared me," she answered. Addison's heart crashed against her chest like ocean waves breaking on the rocks.

"Scared you? All I did was call," Chris replied with a chuckle.

"I was listening to something that freaked me out," she admitted.

"What are you listening to?" His voice perked up, evidencing his enthusiasm for freak-out-inducing materials and matter.

"It's some tape I found in my patient's stuff, but I can't figure out what the recording is from."

"Are you a little sticky bandit? Why do you have your patient's stuff?"

"He made me promise to take his things before he died, and since he has no family or anything, I brought it home."

"I'm sorry, I didn't realize he had passed." Chris's voice softened.

"It's okay."

"So, should I come over so you can play the tape for me? I'm good at identifying obscure songs."

"You think you're so slick, don't you." Addison's shoulders relaxed.

"I know I am," he laughed.

When he arrived, they kissed, and it was like second nature. He draped his faded blue coat over the back of the couch and kicked off his high-top Vans, revealing mismatched socks. He always wore some iteration of Carhartt work pants and a solid colored T-shirt. The epitome of blue collar. Addison sparked another blunt for them to share. Together they cozied up in front of the tape deck, toes digging into the orange shag carpet. A waft of warm air settled around them as the heat kicked on with a click and a growl. After a quick rewind, Addison played the cassette tape for him.

"Number nine, number nine . . ."

It took only seconds for him to recognize it. Not surprising for someone who listened to classic rock almost incessantly.

"That's that weird Beatles song." He snapped his

fingers as though they'd help him remember. "Uhhhh . . . 'Revolution 9.'"

Addison nodded in agreement. "That's right; I knew it sounded like a voice I've heard before. John Lennon."

"You think that's creepy? Imagine what it would sound like backwards," Chris said, inhaling a puff of smoke. Upon exhaling, he blew a series of smoke rings like the Cheshire Cat. It was his signature party trick, one that still managed to impress Addison.

Wheels began spinning in her head. "Can we do that on this tape player?" she asked. He shrugged, then pulled out his phone. A quick Google search and two videos later, they figured out how to play the cassette in reverse, which, as promised, was *much* creepier.

"Turn me on, dead man; turn me on, dead man . . ." The voice and accompanying piano were beyond ominous now. Addison's blood ran cold.

"Okay, turn it off," she demanded, leaning into Chris's muscular arms. Her hand slid onto his calloused elbow as she pushed his embrace tighter around her. Tickled by his long blond beard, she repositioned her head. Chris reached to hit the pause button without letting go, then switched the player over to the radio.

"You're listening to 93.2 WROQ, Maine's number-one rock station," the disc jockey announced. Chris lowered the volume. His paint-speckled hand slid into Addison's. It was rough and thick against her palm. Their fingers laced together.

"How was work?" Addison asked.

"Not bad. We started working on a new housing

development this week, Royal Redlands. We starting building, but there was some sort of hiccup with an investor, so they paused the job for today and sent us all home early. It worked out, though. I was able to catch some waves before it got too late."

"Who comes up with these housing development names?" Addison laughed. "I'm glad you were able to surf. Have you decided if you're going to compete next summer? I can be your surfing groupie."

"I'm strongly leaning toward competing. Now, if you promise to be my groupie, then I'm definitely going to have to sign up. Can't pass up that opportunity." He smiled. "I need to get you out there; you'd be so hot on a longboard."

"I don't know about that. I'll just cheer you on from the comfort of my beach umbrella. I'm not trying to get eaten by a shark." Addison shuddered at the thought.

"You're more likely to get struck by lightning." He laughed and squeezed her even tighter.

A moment of silence gripped them.

"It's that time again, listeners," the disc jockey declared. *"B Sides before Midnight."* Despite his suave inflection, the words did not rhyme.

Addison and Chris shot each other a conspiratorial glance.

"What's on the other side of the tape?" Chris asked, nudging Addison back into reality. By this time, her eyes were becoming too heavy to keep open.

"I'm not sure, I haven't checked," she said, sitting up.

Curious fingers flipped the tape to side B and pressed play.

A voice began speaking, but the words were incomprehensible and rather eerie. It was a garbled mess of sounds.

"This actually sounds like it was intentionally recorded backward," Chris said as he rewound the tape before playing it in reverse.

Static emanated from the speakers for a moment, then a crackle. Heavy breathing erupted. A voice began speaking in a low, pressured tone.

"I don't have much time. The people that are after me are dangerous, and they won't stop until I am dead. You have to finish what I started." The voice paused, panting into the microphone. "I've left clues for you, Addison. Follow the yellow brick road. These people are evil and demonic. Darkside must die." The microphone dropped with a thud, causing Addison to throw her hands over her ears. A distant grappling came within earshot. Grunting, yelling, and slamming. Something crashed to the ground. Something heavy. Someone picked up the microphone. A different individual panted, then the sound cut off. The rest of the tape was blank.

Addison eyes widened. She swallowed hard as she attempted to process what she had just heard.

"I'm not crazy, right? He did say my name," Addison stammered.

"I definitely heard your name," Chris replied, turning off the tape deck. Addison turned around to face Chris, wrapping her legs around him and nuzzling her face into his shoulder.

"I don't understand; how is this is even possible? I'm too high for this right now."

"I honestly don't either. Could it be some sort of prank?" Chris stroked her back.

"No. No way. He died." Addison's breath quickened. "Not in that exact moment, but still as a result of a gunshot wound. Someone dangerous was really after him, but I just don't see how I'm involved in this. How could he have known my name before he was even my patient?"

"Hey, look at me." Chris gripped her shoulders. "Just breathe; it's going to be okay. Should I call the police?"

"Yes," Addison said, still working to regulate her breath, then stopped him with a gentle hand. "Wait, no. I could lose my nursing license if they find out I took his belongings home." Paranoia set in.

"How, though? He told you to take his stuff, right?"

"Yes. I can't prove that, though," Addison said. "I need more time to figure this out when I'm clearheaded."

"Does anyone else know you have his stuff?"

"I don't think so." Addison searched her memory. "No one saw me take it. At least not that I know of."

"Okay, good, so I think we're okay right now." Chris pulled her back into his arms and brushed a loose strand of hair behind her ear. "Everything is going to be okay. We'll figure this out when we're sober."

Chris began to massage Addison's neck, then her shoulders and back. Her nerves calmed. Tension melted away at his touch. He scooped her up, taking her into the bedroom. Their bodies melded between the sheets, pleasantly brief but intoxicating.

A kiss sealed the night. Addison didn't want to let go, but Chris had to be to work in a few hours. Their hands separated slowly until only their fingertips touched and he was gone. She settled back into her bed, looking at her phone one last time before rolling over to fall back asleep.

MESSAGE FROM UNKNOWN

Perplexed, Addison opened the text.

UNKNOWN

Turn me on dead man.

Panic welled up inside of her. Possibilities raced through her mind. It had to be Chris messing with her— that was the only reasonable explanation.

ADDISON

Very funny, Chris

No reply.

She swiped over to her texts with Chris.

ADDISON

Nice one, Chris

CHRIS

??

ADDISON

That anonymous text you just sent me

CHRIS

What anonymous text?!

ADDISON

I know it was you, "Turn me on dead man"

CHRIS

Go to sleep, you're tired.

FIVE
HANNAH

OCTOBER 30, 1976

HANNAH PEELED her eyes open and thrust her hands to her head, cradling it, yet with each movement her head throbbed more. When she removed her hands, she noticed a black residue. After another confirmative swipe, she pilled the black sludge between her thumb and index finger. Paul's wrinkled Pink Floyd shirt still shrouded her body. It smelled of beer and incense. Where was she? A jolt of panic shot through her chest as she scanned her surroundings. Even the panic caused her head to throb. The cement floor was cold against her bare feet. Her body had been placed several rows from center stage.

Goose bumps covered her bare arms as she stumbled down the aisle. Each slow step down brought with it a hammerlike pounding in her head. Scrambling onto the stage, she searched for any remnants of the night before. There were none, not even the faintest dripping of candle wax. Could she have imagined everything? Was it all just a bad trip? The backwards music, the chanting, the dagger. She clutched her neck as she recalled the blade that pressed firmly against her skin, slicing into her flesh and drawing a trickle of blood. Flakes of crusted blood dusted her fingertips.

Hannah gulped. Visions of Paul and his friends circling her and towering above her flashed through her mind. She pressed her eyes shut. Sunlight burned red through her eyelids as she remembered what Jane had said. They were planning to kill her. Hannah cradled her aching head in her hands, sitting in the very spot she had blacked out in. What was it Paul had said? She was chosen? Chosen for what?

Hannah endured a short but painful journey home. To her dismay, her mother's car was still in the driveway, foiling her plans to sneak inside unnoticed. Her mom must have found out that she hadn't stayed over at Carrie's. Hannah flipped the Pink Floyd shirt inside out to conceal the band logo before stepping inside with caution.

"Hannah, is that you?" her tearful mother shouted, emerging into the hall, her eyes dark from lack of sleep. A crumpled-up tissue was glued to her hand.

"Yes, Mom, it's me." Hannah fought to slow her heartbeat as a wave of nausea washed over her.

"I was worried sick." Her mom dabbed her nose with the tissue.

"I'm fine. I was at . . ."

"Don't you dare lie to me. Don't you dare say you

were at Carrie's, because Carrie called me last night to ask if you'd come home."

"I wasn't going to say Carrie." Hannah searched for an excuse. "Look, Mom, in all honesty, Carrie ditched me to have sex with her boyfriend. I didn't feel comfortable, so I went off on my own and ended up making some new friends."

"Shameful." Her mother clutched her imaginary pearls. "Are you hungover?" She sniffed around Hannah like a drug dog.

"No, Mom." Hannah pulled away.

"You reek, Hannah." Her mother stomped out of the room for a moment, letting doors slam behind her, then returned with a religious pamphlet. "You have eight hours to pack your bags, Hannah Jean. When I get back from work, I am dropping you off at this camp. They have a wonderful rehab program. Lord knows you need it."

"I'm not going to a Catholic drug camp."

"I don't want to hear it, Hannah." Her mom slammed the pamphlet onto the entryway table. "You are going, and that is the end of it." She scooped up her purse and keys, then stormed out. Somewhere in the midst of their altercation she had managed to throw on a pantsuit and heels. After looking at the kitchen clock, Hannah guessed her mother would only be a half hour late to work after all.

Hannah chugged a glass of Alka-Seltzer and took a cold shower. In the cozy breakfast nook, she sipped away the final remnants of her hangover with a freshly brewed cup of black coffee. Her mother's brew was never strong enough.

The phone began to ring. It was far too soon for a packing update. Maybe it was Carrie, Hannah thought. She leaned back to grab the green-corded phone from the wall mount.

"Hello?"

". . ."

"Hello? Who is this?"

". . ."

"Carrie, is that you? Why would you tell my mom that I didn't stay with you?"

"Are you tired of living by your mother's incessant rules?" a resonant voice bellowed.

"Who is this?" Hannah pressed the phone closer to her ear.

"What if I told you I could give you everything you have ever wanted?"

"I'm serious, if you don't tell me who you are, I am going to hang up."

"Do you want to be beautiful like your friend Carrie? Clear, tan skin. A feminine figure. Do you want to wear whatever clothes you desire? Go wherever you want to go? Listen to whatever music you want to listen to? Date any man you'd like? Escape the clutches of your mother?"

Hannah remained silent.

"That sounds nice, doesn't it?" the deep voice taunted.

"Even if I did want those things, none of that is possible."

"Oh, but it is possible, especially when you're chosen."

Hannah froze. "Ch-chosen? Chosen for what?"

"Chosen to receive, Hannah. You can have all of those things and more, if you choose to join us."

"Who is *us*? And what if I don't want to?"

"There are always consequences to every choice, whether good or bad."

"That doesn't really answer my question."

"A car will be by to pick you up in thirty minutes. The choice is yours. If you choose to become a receiver, get in the passenger's seat, and you will be rewarded."

"Is this Paul?" With the green telephone cord stretched into the living room, she climbed onto the back of the flower couch and spread the blinds open just enough to scan the street.

"What have you got to lose, Hannah?"

With a click, Hannah's ear filled with the melodic pulse of the disconnect tone.

In exactly thirty minutes, Hannah heard the roar of an engine revving outside. Her heart raced. She carefully pried open the blinds once more, her knees digging into the couch cushion. A black Pontiac Firebird with gold accents idled in her driveway, dominating the otherwise quiet street. She looked back at the pamphlet taunting her from the entryway. Her mother's threat echoed in her mind. Adrenaline surged through her body as she faced a crossroad. She had never been chosen for anything. Not for the cheerleading squad. Not for prom queen. And certainly not to be anyone's girlfriend.

Gazing into the entryway mirror, she felt repulsed by her acne-covered face and unkempt eyebrows. Could she somehow become attractive? Desired? Confident? *Chosen?*

She snatched her leather jacket from the coatrack and bolted for the passenger's side of the car. From the driver's seat, Paul turned to face Hannah, a smile carved deep into his handsome face. With one hand gripping the gearshift, he said, "Rule number one, Hannah. Murder isn't about violence, and it's not about lust. It's about possession. The ultimate possession is the taking of a life. And then there are the physical possessions you gain as a result. What possession will you gain first?"

SIX

ADDISON

THANKSGIVING DAY

A FRESH POT of coffee brewed in the kitchen, cutting the cold November air with the scent of warm roasted coffee beans and a hint of hazelnut. Addison leaned her hip against the chipped kitchen counter, her short black hair a mess after a night of tossing and turning. Her sore hands cradled a mug that read *Stay Golden*—a gift from Veronica one Christmas, or maybe it was a birthday, as an ode to their favorite television show. Veronica was Blanche to Addison's Dorothy, as fun loving and promiscuous as Addison was tough and compassionate. When Norah was adopted into the friendship, she was dubbed the Sophia of the bunch, quick witted, kooky, and loving.

Addison's green-and-blue plaid robe fell open, revealing Chris's boxers from the night before and a faded Nirvana *Nevermind* T-shirt. Her mind wandered to the mysterious text message. She was still unsure if Chris was the culprit, though he typically wasn't one to play games. It seemed especially odd after everything that had happened the night before.

Addison sat at the dining room table, sipping her unsweetened coffee. The PATIENT BELONGINGS bag was still out in the open, the tape still in the deck. She felt a twinge of unease. If the text really was from someone *unknown*, should she be leaving everything so vulnerable?

She thought about her patient. What if *he* was bad? Schizophrenic? His deep, pressured voice replayed in her mind. *Addison.* He knew her name. He'd known her name before he knew *her*. It had to be a coincidence. Norah would likely have some valuable insight. Addison decided to bring her friend up to speed, and Norah replied quickly.

NORAH

Based on what you've told me, I don't think he's schizophrenic. For sure a little eclectic. The wizard of oz references are odd, but he had the actual book with him. For some reason, it seems like he wants you to uncover something. Whatever he's hiding.

One sec, I'm going to change your contact name to Nancy Drew.

ADDISON

Ugh, ok thanks. I just don't understand. Why me?

NORAH

That's the million dollar question.

What kind of alligator does detective work?

ADDISON

Norah, this isn't the time for jokes

NORAH

Come on

ADDISON

I don't know, what kind

NORAH

An investiGATOR

ADDISON

Haha, very funny

NORAH

You know that was a good one ;)

Stay safe, I'll see you at Mrs. Wells' later

Frigid air kissed Addison's rosy cheeks as she made the trek across the street to Mrs. Wells's house—a trek she had made on almost every major holiday since her mom left. Her hair was now brushed and styled into a sleek French bob, a touch of red lipstick dabbed onto her lips and cheeks. A brown trench coat hugged her petite figure.

Mrs. Wells's house was drenched in art nouveau, with round windows accented by green metal. Statues of women, which Addison had always thought resembled goddesses, guarded the lawn. Whimsical floral motifs were scattered and swirled about the exterior of the house. Daisies had been intricately woven through two trellises that flanked a medieval wooden front door.

Before she could even knock, the door burst open and a heavy wave of incense spilled from inside, crashing into Addison and filling her nostrils with a familiar tingle. Patchouli and cedar. Open arms adorned in silver jewelry pulled her in for an embrace that warmed her stomach. Mrs. Wells's hair had gone gray now, though it was still braided and secured in her signature red hair tie. The wrinkles etched into her face formed a poem that spoke of both despair and delight. Her pale eyes twinkled with a spark of joviality.

Distant echoes of laughter welcomed Addison inside.

Every room of the two-story house had distinct and elaborate wallpaper. Bold colors. Crown molding. In the entryway, glass curio cabinets housed various collections of crystals, rocks, and figurines from around the world, treasures that boasted of a life well traveled.

The pleasant and comforting smell of Thanksgiving dinner lured Addison toward the dining room. Friends and family were already gathered, some catching up while others helped put the final touches on the antique dining table. The food and serving ware were laid out elegantly, everything looking photo ready for an Anthropologie catalog. Addison took note that the dining chairs had been reupholstered since the last time she was there; deep-crimson velvet had replaced the white florals. She gave Mrs. Wells a nod of approval.

"Hi, babe," Veronica said as she set down a steaming

bowl freshly baked rolls. The skirt of her hand-sewn pinup dress twirled gracefully as she moved. She leaned in to hug Addison, her scent lingering long after release. Vanilla and caramel.

"Happy Thanksgiving," Addison said, making her rounds. A couple of Mrs. Wells's girlfriends, Ms. Alora and Ms. Torosyan, paused their heated gossip session to offer a kind finger wave from across the table. They too were quite eclectic and colorful. Though Addison only ever saw them on the holidays, they were Mrs. Wells's favorite traveling buddies and part of almost every adventurous tale she told.

Before sitting down, Addison received a tight squeeze from Veronica's parents, who still lived down the street. Even though Addison and Veronica hadn't officially become best friends until they were in junior high, they'd grown up on the same block. It was obvious that Veronica had inherited her fierce beauty from her father, Emmanuel. Even as a middle-aged man with skin leathered by the sun, he managed to ensnare many a woman's gaze with his piercing eyes and killer smile. Though equally beautiful, Veronica's mother was soft and simple. Mrs. Gonzales kept her slim frame covered modestly and rarely wore any makeup. She didn't need it.

"So, how does it feel, mija? Veronica told us yesterday was your last day," Mrs. Gonzales asked as everyone began serving themselves.

"Bittersweet," Addison answered. Mr. Gonzales gripped her shoulder, giving it a consolatory squeeze. His hands were stained black from years of working as a mechanic.

"If you need a little vacation, we're planning a girls' trip to Thailand next month," Ms. Torosyan enthused as she pressed a knife full of butter into her roll.

"We could use our frequent-flier points to get you a ticket. Just say the word," Ms. Alora added.

Mrs. Wells beamed in agreement.

"Thank you. I might take you up on that," Addison admitted. "I haven't really decided what I want to do next, but I do really need to take a break from bedside nursing for a while."

"You've had a rough year," Veronica noted. "Well, several years, with COVID and everything. I think your body and mind deserve a break."

"Honey, is Norah stopping by?" Mrs. Wells asked as everyone scraped the last remnants of food from their plates. Just as Veronica popped the cork of a second bottle of sauvignon blanc, there was a knock on the door.

"Sorry I'm late." Norah shuffled into the dining room wearing surgical scrubs and tie-dye crocs. Her entire wardrobe was made up of scrubs and sweats, and her thick curls were unruly even when she attempted to tame them. Her skin was covered with as many freckles as stars in the night sky. Always in a hurry, she was never on time.

"It's quite all right, honey. I'm so glad you were able to make it," Mrs. Wells said, preparing Norah's plate while she quickly said hi to everyone.

After Norah scarfed down her meal and the table

was communally cleared, everyone made their way into the living room to finish their wine. The room was bright and airy, filled with more than enough comfortable seating and pillows. It was the least vibrant room in the house but the most welcoming.

Addison's and her two friends sat close together on one end of the sectional couch.

"How are things going with Chris?" Norah asked, nibbling on her third dinner roll.

"Really well, actually," Addison said. "He makes me feel safe, and I honestly enjoy just being with him even if we aren't really doing anything."

"Why are you making that face, then?"

"I just don't understand why he hasn't asked me to be his girlfriend yet."

"She's been talking to another guy too," Veronica announced, garnering the attention of listening ears.

"Is this true, Addison?" Ms. Torosyan shifted to face the girls.

"Yes." Addison smiled, gently puffing her chest. "Until Chris and I are officially exclusive, I am going to keep exploring my options."

"Tell us everything." Mrs. Wells sat at the edge of her seat.

"I have a better idea," Norah said after swallowing the last bite of her roll and brushing the crumbs from her top. "Screen mirror your phone to the TV so we all can see what he looks like."

"No way," Addison blurted.

"Oh, come on," Ms. Torosyan and Ms. Alora harmonized, swooning for the entertainment.

"You don't have to do anything you don't want to, mija," Veronica's mom honeyed.

"To heck with that. We want to see him," Mr. Gonzales gleamed, giving Addison his rapt attention.

Before Addison could say anything else, Mrs. Wells turned the television on and Norah snatched Addison's cell phone.

"You really should change your passcode," Norah said, unlocking the phone with ease.

Casablanca Notifications

You have received 1 new message from Tye

Norah navigated to the dating app, which was now on full display across Mrs. Wells's sixty-inch television screen. Veronica had disappeared momentarily but reemerged with a bottle of wine to top everyone off.

"Give me that." Addison glared at Norah, snatching her phone back. "I'll do the scrolling."

Addison opened Tye's Casablanca profile, eliciting a few oohs and aahs. The first picture was a black-and-white professional headshot, though it could have easily been from a modeling portfolio. A quick bio revealed he was over six feet tall, worked in tech, drank socially, and was looking for something serious. A prompt asked *What is the craziest thing on your bucket list?* His answer: *To see Heaven's Gate Mountain.* A series of hiking photos followed, all featuring his blissful border collie.

"He seems to live a very active lifestyle," Mrs. Wells stated.

"He must have rock-hard abs," Mr. Gonzales asserted.

"Should I open the new message?" Addison asked, despite knowing the answer.

"Of course," Veronica hollered, gripping Norah's hand in anticipation.

TYE

I know it's Thanksgiving, but I can't wait much longer to take you out on an official date. There's this really cool piano bar I've been dying to check out, it's called Careless Whisper. If you are up to it, let's meet there at 9 pm tonight.

It was just after six, and by the look of fascination on everyone's face, Addison knew she had to say yes.

Suddenly, a loud crash echoed through the house. A symphony of shattered glass pierced the air. Then a sharp scream erupted.

Addison and Norah reflexively jumped to their feet and ran toward the bloodcurdling scream. It was coming from the entryway. As they approached, they found shards of glass scattered in disarray. Ms. Alora sat on the floor in bewilderment, blood trickling from her hand and tears in her eyes. Her breath stuttered as she tried to catch it. She must have slipped out while everyone was focused on Addison's love life.

The girls were careful to avoid stepping on glass as they worked their way over to Ms. Alora.

"What in the world?" Mrs. Wells cried.

"Ronnie, grab me some paper towels," Addison shouted, sending Veronica running toward the kitchen.

After cleaning the area, they discovered the wound wasn't as bad as it looked. A small but deep cut ran along the base of Ms. Alora's thumb.

"How did this even happen?" Norah asked, pushing some of the glass aside with her croc.

"It was an accident," Ms. Alora wailed.

"What is that in your purse?" Mrs. Wells asked. Beside Ms. Alora, a tattered blue Birkin gaped, revealing two large shimmering tanzanite crystals.

Ms. Torosyan gasped. "Alora!"

"You really should get to the hospital. You're going to need some stitches," Norah urged while Addison applied pressure to the wound.

Mrs. Wells stomped over the glass, crunching it into smaller pieces beneath her boots, and ripped the crystals from Ms. Alora's purse.

"Those are my crystals," Ms. Alora snarled.

"How did you manage to break the glass?" Norah asked, her expression genuinely curious.

"I lost my balance, and one of the crystals smashed into the glass cabinet," she explained while Veronica's father helped her back to her feet.

The women began bickering.

"And I thought our drama was bad," Norah whispered as she helped Addison and Veronica sweep up the glass.

Mr. Gonzales shuffled the older women toward the door, offering to drive Ms. Alora to the emergency room.

"You better go get ready for your date," Mrs Wells insisted.

"Yes, Addy, go, we've got this," Veronica said as she and Norah continued to clean.

Addison gripped Mrs. Wells's hand. "Are you sure? I can stay longer."

"Nonsense." Mrs. Wells smiled to prove she would be okay.

Addison kissed her on the cheek, then sprinted home, leftovers in tow.

As she mounted the first creaky step of her porch, something caught her eye. An envelope was propped up against the base of her front door. A subtle look over her shoulder revealed nothing out of the ordinary. She scooped up the white envelope, carefully balancing it atop the Tupperware, and went inside, locking the door behind her. The flap wasn't sealed, the adhesive still dry. Inside was a small piece of torn printer paper with magazine-clipped letters attached that read:

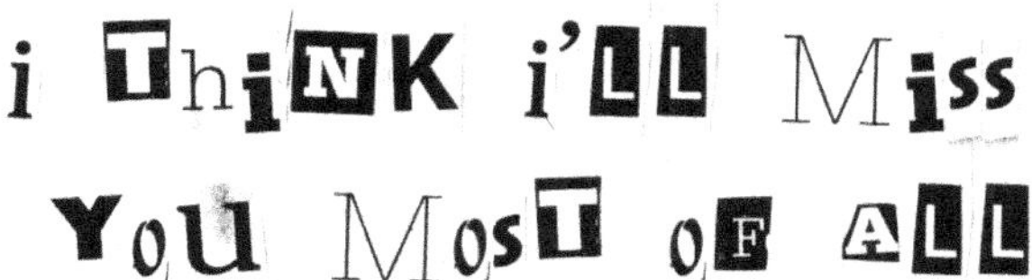

SEVEN
ADDISON

ADDISON'S BREATH quickened as she scanned the house to confirm that all the doors and windows were locked. Everything was sealed tight. The key, book, and cassette tape were still where she had left them. An exhale of relief escaped her before she proceeded to hide all of them deep beneath her mattress. She held the mysterious letter in her hand, its edges now slightly crumpled. In that moment, it became clear to her that this wasn't Chris messing around. Somehow, someone knew. She wasn't sure of the extent of what they knew, but someone knew.

Instinct drove her to call Veronica, even though they'd just been together.

"Hey, Addy." Veronica sounded exhausted, having stayed to help Mrs. Wells with the aftermath of Thanksgiving dinner and Ms. Alora's accident.

"Are you home yet?" Addison asked.

"I just left. That was wild, huh? I never expected Ms.

Alora to do something like that. Ms. Torosyan, maybe, but Ms. Alora?"

"How was Mrs. Wells after I left?"

"She's fine. You know how they are with their old-lady drama. They have their little fights, then quickly make up."

"What are you doing the rest of the night?"

"I'm going to finish making some ponche navideño. I'm still in a festive mood."

"Save me some." Addison plopped onto her couch. It was sunset, and the warm, fading sun caught brilliantly in stained-glass artwork that hung in the living room window. Colors danced along the walls.

"What's wrong? You sound weird." Veronica knew Addison well enough to gauge her moods.

"Something strange happened, but I don't know what to make of it," Addison explained.

In a brief moment of silence, she heard Veronica stirring the punch. A wooden spoon clanked against a metal pot. She could almost smell the warm oranges, apples, and cinnamon through the phone.

"What happened?" Veronica asked.

"First of all, I kind of took my patient's belongings home with me," she confessed.

"What the hell, Addy?" Veronica scolded.

"I know, but he made me promise to keep his stuff safe." An unsettling feeling fluttered in Addison's stomach. "I couldn't protect him from dying, but I can protect his stuff from whatever or whoever he was keeping it from."

Veronica gave an agreeable nod. Addison began detailing what was in the bag, the cassette tape recordings, and the mysterious messages she'd received.

"'I think I'll miss you most of all.'" Addison read the paper aloud, shaking off a chill.

"What is that even supposed to mean? Wait, I'll Google it." Veronica went silent for a moment, then she returned. "It's from *Wizard of Oz*. Dorothy whispers that exact line to the scarecrow before leaving Oz."

"Clearly this is a theme in whatever's going on," Addison declared. "But why would this unknown person choose those specific words for me?"

"I don't know, Addy. This is getting freaky. What if someone is planning to hurt you?" Veronica asked.

"Over what, though?"

"I don't know, Addy, you said yourself that the guy addressed you by your name on the recording, and now someone is stalking you?"

"Well, when you put it that way . . ." Addison began.

"There's no other way to put it," Veronica said. "Whatever clues he left you must lead to something important. Are you going to go to the police? Your patient told you that these people are dangerous—whoever they are."

"No, not yet at least," Addison said. "Everything is super creepy, but as of now if I go to the police, all I can tell them is that I stole my patient's stuff and someone left me a mildly threatening letter on my doorstep. I can't risk getting myself in trouble unless and until I have enough proof that someone is even trying to harm me."

"I guess you're right," Veronica agreed reluctantly.

"Let's stop talking about this," Addison requested as she made her way back upstairs to her bedroom. Unlike the rest of the house, the room was plain, with white hotel-esque bedding, walnut flooring, and matching midcentury modern furniture. Like the rest of the house, it had plants tucked in every corner, spilling from shelves like waterfalls and lined along the windowsill like the queen's Royal Guard.

Two shifts in the ICU as a new grad nurse had compelled Addison to buy a book on feng shui. Her sanity depended on making her bedroom a sanctuary. Posters came down, blue shag carpet was ripped out, and leopard-print bedding was tucked away for the Goodwill, all in a night's work. Conceptually, it was brilliant, but in reality it still took something synthetic, illicit even, to tame her anxiety-induced insomnia. After receiving the cryptic messages of late, she found herself thankful she had put her bed in command position.

"I have to start getting ready for my date with Tye tonight," Addison said as she fingered through the dresses in her closet. "I'm not sure if it's a jeans-and-boots kind of place or more of a dress-and-heels situation."

"Definitely jeans and boots," Veronica suggested. "I've been once or twice—it's supercute. It's like Coyote Ugly meets the Big Easy."

Together they settled on an outfit that hugged Addison's body in all the right places. Her worn leather jacket was the cherry on top. With a "Bye, babe," Veronica signed off, and by 9:01 Addison was approaching the colossal doors of Careless Whisper.

"Addison?" a voice graveled from behind. Boots scraped against asphalt, and Addison looked up—about six feet five inches up. Deep-set eyes imbued the man's face with a mysterious quality that had not come off in his pictures. The photos also had not captured the intensity of his jawline, which sat beneath a soul-crushing smile terminating in two deep lines on either corner of his mouth. His face was a delectable meal seasoned with stubble.

"You must be Tye." Addison extended her hand but instead found herself pulled in for a hug. Her heart raced almost as much as her mind, which was a muddle of both clean and dirty thoughts—mostly dirty. The cold left her body, his embrace leaving her warm long after he released her. She wasn't supposed to feel this attracted to him.

"I'm excited to check this place out," Tye said as he held the door open for Addison. Indistinct chatter, glasses clanking together in celebratory cheers, tinkling piano keys, and the ascending edge of a saxophone echoing into the parking lot pulled them inside like a vortex. The bar extended across the length of the back wall. Bottles of liquor reached to the ceiling, backlit in warm yellow light. In the center of the bar, individual red light bulbs boldly spelled out CARELESS WHISPER.

Round wooden tables speckled the room, all of them occupied and littered with drinks. Disco balls hung from the rafters, reflecting squares of light in every direction.

Opposite the bar was a stage with two grand pianos, each with their own tip and request jars. Scarlet curtains cascaded in the background.

Tye gripped Addison's hand, dragging her through the crowd toward the bar. His palm was soft and smooth against hers. A spot opened up and he made a beeline toward it, their hands still welded together.

"What would you like?"

"Blue Moon," she shouted into his ear, as her voice wasn't strong enough to cut through the noise even if she screamed. Her voice, like her stature, was petite. Two fingers shot up and two beers came their way, sweating from the cold. They clanked bottle tops, a preface to their synchronous gulp.

Across the room, fingers danced flamboyantly across the piano keys, hushing the crowd. The other pianist leaned into his microphone and sang the opening bars of "Piano Man."

The crowd roared with excitement and joined in.

With his beer raised overhead, Tye shouted the words along to the melody. He wrapped his other arm around Addison's waist, and they swayed. She became lost in the moment, forgetting everything outside the bar.

Two beers later, the pianist pounded the intro to "Wannabe" by Spice Girls into the keys, and Addison, along with every other millennial woman in the bar, squealed like a schoolgirl as she belted the lyrics.

Tye cheered on her dance moves, which somehow worked despite her lack of rhythm. She bobbed to the music, pointing an index finger at Tye from around her beer bottle while yelling the chorus before taking a big gulp. When a table opened up right in front of the stage, they swooped in, resting their jackets on the backs of the chairs to claim their place.

Hours of dancing, flirting, and singing at the top of their lungs culminated in a voracious kiss. Addison stood on the tips of her toes to reach Tye's mouth. His hand wrapped around the base of her neck, pulling her in deeper. Closer. Her hands gripped the leather of his belt, closing the small gap between them.

"I'll be back." Addison excused herself to the restroom. Sparks threatened to explode into a full-blown fire if she didn't take hold of some distance.

Once she had finished washing her hands, she sauntered back down the dark hallway toward the crowd. The buzz hit harder now that she'd emptied her bladder. She stopped in her tracks, her ears honing in on a sound that was eerily familiar. The ominous, reversed piano tune from the cassette tape swept through the venue, as confident and real as the intro to every other song that had been played. Bracing herself against the wall, Addison took a deep inhale. The motif repeated. She ran back to the crowd, eyes darting toward the pianists. Just as they came into view, the tune dissipated, naturally transitioning into a very different song.

There was pressure on her shoulder, a hand squeezing firmly and authoritatively. She bolted around, crashing into Tye. Her pulse quickened.

"Whoa." He stepped back. "Are you okay? You look like you've seen a ghost."

"I . . ." She paused. "I'm fine. I just thought I heard something."

His brows scrunched together. "What did you think you heard?"

Without answering, Addison darted for the door and slipped into the quiet, cold night. The door sealed the noise and chaos inside as it shut.

Outside, crickets chirped. The white noise of cars in the distance grounded her. The wind brushed an icy kiss against her flushed cheeks. Another squeeze on her shoulder startled her, though this time it was much softer.

"It was nothing," she assured Tye as she looked into his eyes. "I'm really sorry. I had a good time, a great time, but I think I'm going to go home now."

"Did I do something wrong?" he asked, perplexed, as he struggled to zip up his jacket, making her realize she had forgotten hers.

"No, not at all," she promised. "I'm just tired."

Tye pulled her in close. His lips hovered in search of hers, but before their lips could meet, he settled on a hug. Addison took it as a sign of respect for her decision.

"Text me later, okay?" Addison shouted as she hurried away.

EIGHT
ADDISON

LATER THAT EVENING, sobered by a cup of extra-strong black coffee, Addison locked herself in her bedroom. Every dead bolt in the house had been turned, every blind and curtain closed tight. The chair that was designated for lightly worn clothes was shoved strategically beneath the door handle. Confident that everything was secure, she pried open her mattress and retrieved her patient's copy of *The Wonderful Wizard of Oz*. If what he said in his recording were true, there must be a clue inside. Even if there wasn't, she had to start somewhere.

With a tug and the click of a chain, the warm yellow glow of her bedside lamp illuminated her book. She dug her legs deep under her pillowy down comforter, searching for a comfortable position. When she found it, she began examining the book more closely.

The hard cover was white and green, with several castles and stars. Outwardly, the book was in pristine condition. Inside, however, pages were marked and bent.

As she flipped through the yellowed and stained pages, a small cipher fell onto her comforter. It had been torn from an old Rolodex, its holes frayed. On the outer edge, a tab was labeled X.

The cipher was covered in a series of numbers, all handwritten in fine print:

1-9-1, 24-6-3, 45-6-7, 91-4-2, 119-5-4, 168-6-2, 210-9-5, 291-7-1, 900-4-1, 1231-3-3, 1444-4-2, 1493-7-5, 1618-1-1, 1643-1-2, 1668-4-3, 1668-5-4, 1770-3-6, 1880-9-3, 1893-7-1, 1991-2-3, 1992-3-3, 2110-5-2, 2118-1-1, 2286-7-7, 2407-4-3, 2560-4-2, 2724-4-1, 2888-2-3, 3050-7-2

With a grunt, Addison reached into her nightstand to retrieve her notebook that she always kept close by to write down anything that was bothering her or causing her anxiety before going to bed. However, while she had anxious thoughts almost every night, only a few pages had actually been filled out. Wood scraped as she grabbed a multicolored Hello Kitty pen from the table-top. With her thumb, she slid down the purple lever. It was her favorite color.

Unsure of where to begin, she started Googling ciphers on her phone. She continued revising her search until she came across the Ottendorf cipher, in which each letter of an encrypted message was substituted by three numbers correlating with a single letter inside a book. The first number represented the line of text, the second number referred to the word within that line, and the third number corresponded to the letter from that word.

Addison flipped the book open to chapter 1 and

began counting. The first line, ninth word, and first letter gave her *k*. She jotted it down. Next she counted to the twenty-fourth line, sixth word, and third letter: *e*. After having to start her count over at least three times, she began writing the line number next to each line of text. The book had already been marked up; what was a couple more annotations? She continued until she had written *key opens* on her notepad. A flutter in her stomach quickly turned to nausea as she began imagining what the key could open.

The next page was missing from the book. Flipping through the book, she noticed there were even more missing pages. She shook the book, half expecting them to fall out like the cipher had, but they didn't. Without those pages, the entire count would be off. She slammed the book against her bed, unable to continue until she found the pages. If she found them. Tension gripped her shoulders. After spending over an hour painstakingly deciphering the code, she'd run into a major setback, just as she was feeling like she was onto something.

Somewhere in the comforter, her phone buzzed.

CASABLANCA NOTIFICATION

You have received 1 new message
from Tye

TYE

I feel really bad about how things ended
tonight. If you are okay with it, I'd like to
take you out tomorrow night to make up
for it. There is a really cool cover band
I've been wanting to see. Let me know
what you think.

ADDISON

I'm the one that should be apologizing
for tonight. Despite how things ended, I
was having a really good time. I think
tomorrow night sounds perfect. I'd like a
do-over.

With a swipe, she closed the app and maneuvered to her text messages. *Unknown* glared at her like a bright marquee, drawing her inside. A bold stroke of confidence, or maybe something else entirely, compelled her to send a forthright reply.

ADDISON

What do you want?

Minutes passed without a response. Resting the book across her chest, she considered FaceTiming Veronica. Or perhaps Chris would be the better person to call, but then she would have to mention Tye, which was out of the question. Her eyes grew heavy. Her minimalist wall clock told her it was two a.m. Before she could settle on a decision, she was jerked out of a light sleep by a *buzz, buzz.*

Her phone screen lit up, indicating she had received a new message from Unknown.

Tell me what he said, or someone else
will end up dead.

Addison shot up in bed, sending the book and Hello
Kitty pen flying to the floor with a thud. Her heart and
mind raced.

ADDISON

Leave me alone. I don't know who this is
or how you got my number, but this isn't
funny.

As she waited for a response that never came, the
silence embraced her into a deep sleep The phone she
was so diligently glaring at tumbled from her limp hand
into the bed, sinking into the blankets and pillows.

It was almost noon when she awoke. She plunged her
hands into the bedding, blindly searching for her phone.
The screen lit up, notifying her of several missed calls
and voicemails, none of which were from Unknown.
While none of the numbers were blocked, she didn't
recognize any of them.

Maybe Unknown really is going to leave me alone, she
hoped, though in her gut she knew that to be wishful
thinking. She had something they wanted. Whoever
Unknown was had implied they'd harmed her patient,
and for all she knew they had every intention of doing the
same to her.

Unable to quiet her mental chatter, she dialed her
voicemail. In the limited time it took to connect, she
quickly crafted different responses in case it was

Unknown. She could just say her patient hadn't told her anything, that he had been intubated and unable to talk in the hospital.

"Addison, this is Deputy Johnson. We found you listed as Christopher Cromwell's emergency contact. I'm afraid he's been in a pretty bad car accident and is being transported to Community Hospital."

Addison's heart sank like an anchor in the sea, pulling her downward. Tears filled her eyes, not just because of the accident but also at the realization that she was Chris's emergency contact. She couldn't help but wonder if the accident was a result of her conversation with Unknown. After hanging up, she looked for the time stamp of the voicemail: 2:30 a.m. Her breath caught in her throat.

A foot tangled in the covers as she bolted from her bed, which sent her tumbling into the ground. She kicked her foot free. While she scrambled on the floor, she picked up the book and Hello Kitty pen, tucking them back under the mattress. Addison wiggled on a pair of jeans from the pile of lightly worn clothes she had discarded from the chair onto the floor. She tucked the edge of her oversized tee inside her jeans. Not her most attractive outfit, but it would have to do. Like butter, she slid her cell phone into her back pocket.

After a brief struggle to remove the chair from beneath the door handle, she stumbled into the hall, socks in hand. Hobbling on one foot, she pulled the first sock on. In the midst of catching her balance, her hand pressed against her parents' bedroom door, sending it inward with a crash. It had been years since she'd gone in there. She picked herself up off the floor, brushing the carpet dust from her hands. Even though it made her uncomfortable to be in the room, she used the bed to finish putting on her other sock.

Various knickknacks and framed photos rested on her parent's chunky oak dresser, coated in a thick layer of dust. On the edge, turned slightly toward the door, was a picture frame with the photo displaced. A photo she had forgotten existed. Addison itched to fix it.

Using the bottom edge of her shirt, she brushed a layer of dust away to reveal her dad standing in front of the Miller factory he had worked at. He couldn't have been older than twenty-five. It was the version of him she had always remembered, thin, tan, and hairy, but what she found peculiar was the T-shirt he wore, featuring the Beatles' "Revolution 9." A chill ran down her back as she flipped the frame over. Two of the prongs were already pushed aside. She flicked the remaining prongs away and pried the back open, peeling the photo from the frame to reposition it. On the back of the picture, written in faded black ink, was the date *1984*. In newer, blue ink were the words *The great and terrible Oz.*

Her eyes grew big. Wasn't that what her patient had said? Could this be one of the clues he'd "left" for her? A chill tickled her spine. Had her patient been in her house?

With the picture in hand, she darted back to her room for the *Wizard of Oz* book. She thought if she could find that line inside, perhaps it would bring about more clues. More answers. But it would have to wait. She tucked the photo inside the book before slipping everything into a Redlands School of Nursing tote bag that she hurled over her shoulder. She descended the stairs. The car engine roared to a start, and before it could even warm up, she sped over to the hospital.

Chris was covered in dried blood and bruises. A white cast covered the lower portion of his left leg, which was elevated on a stack of pillows. As she came farther into the cold white room, she let out a sigh of relief: He was not on a ventilator but in fact breathing on his own. The monitor revealed stable vital signs. He was going to be okay. She tucked her hand beneath his and squeezed.

"I'm so sorry, Chris." She broke down, letting her tote bag fall gently to the floor.

"Sorry for what?" His reply was slow and arduous.

His eyes opened, lighting up at the sight of her.

"Addy the Baddy." His voice was weak, but the flirtatious inflection translated.

"I'm so glad you're alive. I was so worried when I heard you had been in an accident," Addison said.

He smiled and gripped her hand tighter.

"Also, I found it very cute that you have me as your emergency contact," she added.

"Does that surprise you?"

"Yeah, a little bit."

"Well, my parents are out of the country right now, and you live in Redlands."

Addison's stomach churned. He had only made her his emergency contact out of convenience.

"What happened?" Addison asked, pulling a chair to the bedside.

"I was driving home from the worksite, and this black car was coming from the other direction. They flashed their brights at me, so I quickly looked to see if my headlights were on, and they were. When I looked back up, they were swerving into my lane. I barely had any time to react. It's kind of a blur, but somehow I hit their back fender and spun out. My car rolled into a ditch on the side of the road, and of course whoever hit me took off. They were probably drunk or on their phone or something."

"That's terrifying, Chris. Did you see what they looked like?"

"No. When they flashed their brights, I couldn't see anything," Chris said. "The cops are investigating, but it's unlikely they'll be able to find them. Why were you saying you're sorry earlier?"

Addison explained the texts she had been receiving from Unknown, the mysterious letter on her porch, and the hidden messages she had found in the book as well as behind the photograph of her dad. Silence gripped him longer than Addison expected.

"Addy, that doesn't make it your fault. It's just a coincidence." He laced his fingers into hers. "This does make me worry about you more, though. Maybe you should just tell them whatever they want to know or just go to the police."

Addison ripped her hand away. "No way." Her posture stiffened. "I owe it to my patient to keep this secret until I can figure out what he was hiding. I couldn't save his life; the least I can do is honor his last wishes." Her eyes welled up for a moment, but she stopped the tears from overflowing. "Plus I can't go to the police, remember? I basically stole his belongings; I would have to admit to that. I'm pretty sure that's illegal. I don't want to risk losing my nursing license. I worked too hard and have come too far to allow that to happen."

"I understand your loyalty, but Addison, whoever Unknown is, they clearly are dangerous," Chris said, his eyes blazing with concern and anger.

"I can protect myself, Chris. I've been doing it for years." Addison realized these were sentiments she found herself saying far too often.

"I know you can." His energy seemed to be fading. "Look, I know you're capable of handling yourself—it's one of the qualities I admire most about you—but please tell me everything that's going on so I can help. If they message you again, I want to know everything."

Addison's gaze remained rigid.

"Promise me."

She folded like a losing hand. "I promise."

Their pinkies locked, and with his remaining energy, he pulled her in for a kiss. Wiry hairs tickled her lips. Even with dry, chapped lips, he was a good kisser.

Addison remained by his side as he drifted back to sleep. Metal rings scraped as she tugged the privacy curtain closed and emptied the contents of her tote onto Chris's bedside table. With her legs crossed beneath her on the chair, she began searching the *Wizard of Oz* book for the line "I am Oz, great and terrible." It wasn't too long before she found it on page 96. Much to her astonishment and dismay, the margins of the page were filled with more encrypted numbers in the same format as the Rolodex cipher. Upon further inspection, she noticed a small asterisk in front of a number sequence that began on the lower left side of the page. Following along the outer edge, the numbers wrapped around the top and down the right side. She carefully scribbled each number into her notebook:

3-3-3, 3-2-1, 4-1-2, 5-4-2, 5-7-2, 5-8-3, 7-6-8, 7-6-3, 7-6-4, 7-5-3, 10-6-1, 10-7-4, 10-10-2, 11-4-3, 12-2-1, 12-4-2, 12-5-3, 12-6-1, 13-1-2

Addison let out a sigh that deflated her shoulders before getting to work deciphering. Beginning from the phrase in question, she counted each line, word, and letter until she came up with an address:

Two One Four W Caldetto

NINE
HANNAH

OCTOBER 30, 1976

"MY MOM WILL BE HOME in six hours," Hannah said as she tore a loose piece of skin from her thumb with her teeth. The taste of blood, warm and metallic, filled her mouth.

"Don't worry, I'll have you home in three." Paul winked.

Heat filled the cab of the car, blasting from the vents and mixing with the cold air that flowed freely between the open windows. The Beatles' *White Album* danced from the speakers, transitioning into the melancholy cry of "While My Guitar Gently Weeps." Hannah's gut twisted with a sense of danger, but she breathed it away and breathed in the sweet smell of vanilla and sweat that drifted from Paul's golden skin. She imagined her fingers were the wind in his hair, gliding through the long chestnut tresses that fluttered just enough for her to catch a glimpse of his thick sideburns and strong jaw. Her heart raced with fear and desire as he licked his lips and pressed a cigarette to his mouth. For a moment, a cloud of smoke obstructed her view. When it cleared, Paul's grin was diabolical.

Hannah knew she wasn't pretty enough for Paul. Slightly too young. Way too inexperienced. But if what she had been told was true, she could *become* pretty enough. Cost unknown. The voice had said she could have whatever she desired, and more than being pretty and free of acne, what she desired was for Paul to want her.

They drove east for a little over thirty minutes into the wilderness. Paul parked his car just off the beaten path on a dirt road. Like a gentleman, he opened the passenger door and escorted Hannah from the car.

"Right this way." He gave her a minute to climb out, then slammed the door.

Dirt crunched beneath them until they began mounting a grassy hill, nothing in sight but nature. Birds chirped and crowed. Leaves rustled in the wind. Hannah panted heavily as they climbed, surrounded by wild-flowers.

"Where are you taking me?" she asked.

"Be patient, we're almost there." He extended a masculine hand toward Hannah, which she gladly accepted. His forearm flexed beneath a silver cuff bracelet as he pulled her farther into the wilderness until the trees engulfed them.

"Your first test—" he began, but she cut him off.

"There's going to be more than one test?" Hannah's breath quickened again.

"Yes, Hannah, this is the first of many." Paul lifted the flared bottom of his fitted jeans and retrieved a dagger from his boot. "Can I trust you, Hannah?"

"I-I don't know," she stuttered.

His eyes narrowed. "I can take you home right now, and we can forget this ever happened. You won't ever see me again." He stepped away from her, squeezing the dagger tighter. "Is that what you want, Hannah?"

"No, it's okay, you can trust me."

Paul shoulder's slackened and he approached her, placing the dagger into her hand and gently wrapping her fingers around the hilt. An image of Paul and his friends circling beyond the roaring flames of candlelight flashed into Hannah's mind, but she quickly blinked it away. She realigned her focus on Paul. On the dagger.

"Wh-what do you want me to do?"

"Have you ever killed anything, Hannah?"

She swallowed hard. "A bug, maybe, but not on purpose."

Paul laughed. "All right, looks like I get to experience another first with you. If we keep this up, who knows what other firsts it might lead to?"

Hannah's pulse raced. Sweat beaded her forehead and hands as she followed Paul into a clearing, where a deer had already been trapped. Her heart sank.

"Go ahead." Paul nudged her closer. "Let me see you make your first kill."

"But I thought I was chosen," Hannah stalled. "Why do I have to go through tests if I'm chosen?"

Paul laughed. "Being chosen isn't that simple. While

you are marked and set apart, you must also choose. By completing the tests, you are revealing your choice and taking your rightful place."

Hannah swallowed. "What if I choose not to?"

Paul took a step closer, his body stiffening. "Well, Hannah, I think you already know the answer to that question."

He nudged her closer. Hannah tripped over her feet as she approached the tired deer. Its leg was gnarled and caught in a trap. While Hannah felt sick to her stomach at the thought of harming the animal, her heart ached to put it out of its misery.

"I'm sorry," she whispered as she gripped the dagger with two hands and thrust it into the deer's neck. Blood splattered as she ripped the blade from its flesh, then sank it back in with more force until the deer ceased to move.

"Taste your kill," Paul said, swiping blood from the blade onto his index finger and placing it in Hannah's mouth. It saturated her tongue. "It is now a part of you, and you two are forever one."

Paul dropped to his knees, taking the dagger from Hannah's shaking hands. Without pause, he pressed the blade into the deer's chest, working to remove the heart. Fluids splashed as he tugged the organ free. He plopped it into Hannah's hands. Blood dripped from her palms as she awkwardly held the heart in front of her, scurrying to keep up with him while tears trailed down her cheeks.

They soon approached a small, dilapidated shack. Once a lively summer haven for camp kids, it was now long abandoned. Paul held the door open for Hannah, locking it behind them.

The wooden room was empty except for a circle of candles in the center of the floor. Paul assisted Hannah into the circle, the deer heart still cradled in her grasp.

"Just do as I say," Paul ordered. He lit all the candles and began to chant:

Reviecer eht emoclew

Reviecer eht emoclew

Reviecer eht emoclew

"Repeat this chant and take a bite of the heart," Paul ordered.

"I-I don't know." Hannah hesitated, fighting to hold back more tears.

Paul's eyes filled with rage. "If you do it, you have everything to gain. If you don't . . ." He dragged his thumb across his neck.

"Reviecer eht emoclew." Hannah spoke softly.

"Say it with confidence. Louder."

"Reviecer eht emoclew," she commanded, and sank her teeth into the heart. The candles flickered. She shuddered at the taste of the organ. Her teeth ripped loose a chunk of the tough, chewy meat, shifting it through her mouth. Gagging, she fought to swallow. Water pooled in her eyes. A single tear dripped down her cheek. Was this the cost of gaining what she desired? Her stomach tightened, ready to hurl everything from inside her.

Paul climbed inside the circle, kneeling beside her. A gentle touch climbed up her spine, then gripped the nape of her neck. With his other hand cradling Hannah's, Paul pulled the heart toward his own mouth. Blood drenched his chin. He moved his hand, placing it against the side of her face, pulling her in close for a kiss. Hannah melted at his lips' touch. They were warm and wet from the blood. Hannah's mouth parted, allowing Paul's tongue to slip in.

"Again," he encouraged, and she complied. "Open yourself to receiving both what you desire and what it wants you to receive." The process was repeated until they had consumed most of the heart, their faces smudged with more blood after every carnal kiss. While chanting, Hannah focused her thoughts on her mom changing her mind about sending her to rehab. She focused on her mom allowing her to stay home without any consequences. She focused on becoming beautiful. Then, from seemingly nowhere, a rapid gust of wind blew out the candles.

Paul brought Hannah back home within three hours, as promised. Every trace of the ritual was washed down the shower drain. When her mom returned home from work, she never mentioned the rehab camp. The pamphlet had vanished. Dinner was prepared and served as usual, and the evening commenced with nary a mention of punishment.

TEN
ADDISON

NOVEMBER 29, 2024

WITH GOOD INTENTIONS, Addison suppressed all of the weird events that had transpired in the days before. A steamy shower helped melt away the tension in her neck and shoulders. It took a hit of her blunt to exhale the rest of her anxiety away, just in time for her to get dressed for her date with Tye. Part of her felt wrong for not canceling. Guilt nibbled at her. Chris was lying in a hospital bed while she was going on a date, planning to have fun. Though, after she'd learned where Tye was taking her, she wasn't sure she would.

They were going to see a rock cover band, which she loved, at the Rusty Tavern, which she hated. The Rusty Tavern lived in infamy in Addison's mind. It had been her mom's favorite bar, the setting of many insignificant flings that made their way home, into the kitchen, and onto the couch. Flings that lasted days and sometimes weeks. Some of which impacted Addison physically in the form of bruises and one time a broken thumb. It had been her first and surprisingly only broken bone, which led her to sardonically rename her thumbs Bob in remembrance of the man himself—"two thumbs up" became "two Bobs up." Even with the tavern's rebrand and new management, its seedy underbelly remained. Miserable men, if you could even call them men, still found shadows to lurk in.

At times, admittedly, the Rusty Tavern had been a blessing, a means to take her mother away and facilitate peace and quiet. Other times it had been a curse. A curse that, ironically and perhaps literally, had taken her mother away forever.

Tye picked Addison up in a burnt-orange Chevy Nova that she would later learn was a 1969 Yenko Deuce. She also learned that it had been passed down to him from his grandfather, who was a mechanic and had made most of his small fortune restoring muscle cars.

"You didn't want to follow in his footsteps?" Addison asked.

"I don't like to get my hands dirty. All of that grease and oil." Tye shuddered. "And you better believe he and my dad will never let me live it down." He paused. "Actually," he revised, "Dad didn't let me live it down until I sold my first start-up and gave him a hefty check; then he changed his tune. I think he may have even used the word *proud* for the first time."

"Wow. I don't know whether to feel happy or sad for you."

An amused chortle escaped him. "It's all good. We actually have a really good relationship now."

"Tell me more about you," Addison requested just as he was slipping an 8-track into the tape deck. She appreciated their mutual love for all things retro.

"What would you like to know?" His voice melted into the song, "Breathe" by Pink Floyd. The melodic twang of a guitar and the steady drumbeat softened as he lowered the volume just enough for them to converse.

"Something I don't already know," she said.

"I don't eat yellow Skittles or yellow M&M's," he said in a matter-of-fact tone.

Addison laughed. "What? Why?"

"It all started when I was a kid. I already wasn't a fan of lemon-flavored things, but my friend and I decided to see how many Lemonheads we could eat in a minute or something ridiculous like that. As you can imagine, I got really sick, and somehow that evolved into me not liking pretty much anything yellow."

"Interesting," she said, turning her head away to conceal her judgment.

Nighttime was her favorite time of day, a time when everything became cold, mysterious, and the soul could breathe freely. A cloak of darkness blurred boundaries, and the nocturnal soundtrack calmed her senses. She took in the sights. Houses, most of which had turned down for the night, passed in a haze. Trees waxed and waned in the wind. Bikes were left unattended.

"Don't act like you don't have a weird quirk," Tye protested.

"Nope, not at all," Addison teased with a smirk.

Tye reached over, his forearm flexing to reveal

muscles Addison hadn't seen since anatomy class in nursing school. He slipped his hand beneath hers, lacing his fingers into hers before pulling her hand over to his lap. He flashed a grin so devilish it could cast a spell on her. His nails were clean and manicured. Unlike Chris, Tye's nails had a sheen.

"Come on, tell me a weird quirk you have," he pleaded.

"Okay, fine. I guess I'll go with this one," Addison began.

"Oh, so there's more than one," Tye quipped.

"That's it, I'm not telling you." Addison zipped her lips closed.

"No, no, I'm sorry, please continue." A smile found its way onto his face as he shifted her hand even closer.

"I won't buy anything new until something has broken. My stove is probably fifty years old. I bought my current TV in 2012 to replace the TV my parents bought in the nineties."

"That's not a quirk; that's just being financially responsible," Tye said.

"Okay, fine, how about this one, then? I can't sleep unless my bedroom door and closet door are completely closed."

"What will happen if they're open?"

"My imagination will run wild and I'll start to believe there's someone or something watching me," Addison said, realizing she was squeezing Tye's hand even tighter. The reality was, someone actually could be watching her now.

Nerves gripped her. She reached over and turned the music back up as he pressed the gas pedal deeper into the floorboard, jolting them backward for a moment before weightless bliss softly returned. Streetlights whisked by in a blur of crimson and honey. Addison cranked the passenger window down to dip her arm in the cool mist of night, a stark contrast to the heat from the air vents.

The car slowed down a dimly lit street plagued by potholes and trash. A mess of electrical wires, some of which slouched under the weight of hanging sneakers, linked the streetlights. They passed a row of barred-up shops with CLOSED signs hanging crooked in their windows—a pawnshop, a thrift store, an adult bookstore. All defiled in graffiti.

Just before they reached next intersection, an old brick building with large neon-green block letters spelling RUSTY TAVERN came into view. Above the font were two yellow-and-white beer mugs tilting in a cheers. The front doors of the establishment had been painted shut and chained together, barring entry from that side. The car lurched as Tye pulled into the back parking lot, bobbling him and Addison loftily from side to side and jostling a pair of fluffy red dice hanging from the rearview mirror.

He cranked the car into park and ordered Addison to wait for him to open her door. His hand in hers, he led her to the back entrance. The only entrance. A narrow rusted security door with black arrows spray-painted around the surrounding brick greeted them. Addison slipped under Tye's outstretched arm as he held the door open for her and they were sucked into the atmosphere that was the Rusty Tavern.

The air was heavy with the smell of cigarette smoke, pretzels, and whiskey, speckled with the faintest notes of body odor. Though it was winter, heat radiated from the crowd, the musical equipment, and the small kitchen. There was no central heating or air conditioning, just an old swamp cooler that made the place barely tolerable in the summer months. Beneath their feet were black linoleum floors, worn down in many places and revealing the flooring from days past—like a half-eaten Jawbreaker. Wood-paneled walls painted a deep shade of green caressed the room. Framed paintings, neon signs, and Polaroid photos of patrons and staff blanketed the walls. Addison didn't even have to look to be certain there were Polaroids of her mom up there somewhere.

Onstage, the band was warming up, breaking the heavy chatter with an occasional microphone screech, cymbal tap, or guitar riff. A loud crash of shattering glass pulled everyone's gaze to the back for a moment. In the brief silence, the bartender gave a wave of apology before bending over to pick up the remnants of a highball glass. Seconds later, voices once again erupted in conversation.

The stage and the bar were on opposite ends of a large room. In between, tall round tables were normally scattered about, but on nights like this only a few remained, enabling the crowd to tightly fill the space. On the back wall were two large archways that led into a smaller game room, where deep-crimson felt lined all but one lonely green pool table. A heavy haze of smoke dampened Addison's view—shadowy figures contorted to perform trick shots. Empty beer bottles littered every table. A narrow walkway carved a path to the bathrooms, which were located at what architecturally would be considered the front of the bar.

Tye squeezed past a diverse mix of bikers, edgy young adults, and old patrons who appeared to have aged along with the bar. He returned to Addison with two Scotches on the rocks. As her fingers wrapped around her cold glass, her stomach became unsettled.

"Is something wrong?" Tye searched Addison's face.

"No, it's just that"—she swallowed hard—"well, this is the bar my mom would always come to, and this was basically her favorite drink. It's just missing the twist."

Color drained from Tye's face. He snatched the drink from Addison's hand.

"I am so, so sorry," Tye pleaded, three fingers lifting from the glass for emphasis. "Now that you mention it, I remember you telling me this. I must have gotten it mixed up."

"It's okay, Tye," Addison assured him.

"No, it's not. I should have remembered," he said as he disposed of the drinks on a nearby table. "Let's start over. What is your drink of choice?"

Addison couldn't help but smile at his attentiveness. "I'll take a Blue Moon with an orange slice."

"Coming right up," he promised. And he delivered. With their drinks in hand, they made their way through the crowd toward the stage, finding narrow gaps to slip through. His tall, firm body guarded her as they maneuvered.

"How's everyone doing tonight?" the singer shouted. He was a tall, lanky man with long blond hair and thick sideburns. The crowd cheered in response.

A small, frumpy man dressed all in black wielded the bass. The guitarist was angular and handsome. He didn't have style—he *was* style. A white T-shirt and jeans were the perfect blank canvas to his Jim Morrison–like appearance. The drummer, in contrast, was studious. He looked like he not only knew music theory but likely taught it professionally. The drum kit, with its matte maple shell, had all the bells and whistles. On keys sat a woman who resembled Yoko Ono to a disconcerting degree.

"We are Releanor Igby," the singer proclaimed as the drummer swept through a drumroll, enticing the crowd to pump their fists.

Their set began with "Whole Lotta Love" by Led Zeppelin. Addison and Tye sipped at their drinks and danced, jubilantly belting out whatever lyrics they knew. At one point, Addison gathered every ounce of confidence she had and shouted out a song request—"Rock and Roll Never Forgets" by Bob Seger and the Silver Bullet Band. Her jaw nearly dropped when they obliged. It dropped even more when the singer's voice flawlessly matched Bob Seger's rasp.

Tye tugged Addison into his arms and kissed the back of her head. His scent was warm and pleasant. Addison closed her eyes as they swayed to the music, her concerns and doubts quelled by the alcohol. As the final notes hung suspended in the air, slowly dissipating into momentary stillness, Addison peeled her eyes open. Tye released his grip just long enough for them to clap, unleashing a comforting wave of Old Spice. It reminded her of Chris. A wave of guilt tickled her stomach.

Piano keys tinkled in an ominous manner, seizing Addison's attention. Taking her prisoner.

"Number nine, number nine, number nine," the singer repeated with an accent.

Chaotic sounds panned between speakers, filling the room with the sound of "Revolution 9" by the Beatles. Addison's heart thrashed against her chest and her stomach sank as she watched the keyboard player laugh and make infant sounds aligning with the backtrack. A nearly empty glass slipped from Addison's sweaty palm, causing a momentary divide in the crowd and some dirty looks.

"I'm sorry, I have to go," Addison yelled to Tye, and ran toward the bathroom.

Panting heavily as she cut through the smoky haze, Addison reached for the bathroom door. The band became muffled as she slammed the door shut. Thrusting her back against it, she rested there a moment. *This can't be happening again,* she thought. Deep inhales and long exhales helped her get through the remainder of the song, her body relaxing some when she heard the band transition into what sounded like a Guns N' Roses song. "Welcome to the Jungle."

Walls tiled in lime offered solace. A row of free-standing white porcelain sinks with exposed piping lined the wall to Addison's left. To her right were three dark-green bathroom stalls covered in a collage of vandalism. Straight ahead, a miniature square window with a deep ledge was cracked just enough to welcome a refreshing breeze.

Addison headed into the first stall, lifting and manipulating the door until she found the sweet spot that enabled the latch to slide across. No seat covers. Tearing away several sheets of toilet paper, she strategically lined the seat. Her head fell into her hands, resting there for a moment. It felt fuzzy, though she was unsure if it was the beer or the anxiety.

Just then, a nearby sound startled her back into fight-or-flight. Addison sat up straight, her ears homing in on the sound. It was that same ominous piano sound from "Revolution 9"; however, this time the quality of the sound was poor, like a ringtone on an old cell phone. It was coming from the next stall over.

"Hello," Addison yelled, rushing to pull her pants up and kick the toilet paper into the bowl. She'd flush later.

Silence. She hadn't heard anyone come in.

"Is anyone there?"

Still nothing.

The door to the bathroom opened gently, just enough to allow music and cheering to filter in. Just long enough for someone to slip out. In a whirlwind, Addison bolted from her stall and into the next. The door slammed open, shaking its metal latch. Addison gasped as she was greeted by a message that wrapped around the toilet seat cover, written in bright-red lipstick.

Find the Ruby Slippers – Flush This

With haste, she kicked the seat cover into the toilet and pressed the handle. The message was sucked away in a swirl.

Just in case, she examined the final stall. Nothing was out of the ordinary. Returning to the mirror, she composed herself. Her hair had begun to frizz from the humidity. She swept a few loose strands of hair back into place and patted her face with a paper towel.

A haze of smoke pulled her from the bathroom back into reality. It was chaotic and loud, taunting her anxiety. Tye rushed over to her, ready to guide her back toward the stage with a gentle extension of his arm.

Addison studied everyone like she was a private detective searching for the ruby slippers. Taking the lead, she slipped her hand into Tye's, tugging him in all different directions. Every foot in the bar was under scrutiny as she sifted through the monotony that was Converse and Doc Martin boots.

They reached the far end of the bar. Shimmering red flats adorned in rubies glistened, reflecting the neon glow of a nearby COCKTAILS SIGN.

Addison's breath skipped as her eyes traveled upward. Black leggings and a black-and-white polka-dot corset.

"You bitch," Addison scolded, plummeting a fist into Veronica's arm.

"Ouch." Veronica rubbed the pain away with a mischievous laugh.

"I am never telling you anything again," Addison swore.

"Oh, come on, I couldn't help it," she chuckled, her eyes shifting toward Tye, who was awkwardly standing behind Addison.

"You must be Tye." Veronica extended her hand, revealing long manicured nails.

"Yes." He smiled, receiving her hand for a shake. Once the pleasantries had been exchanged and Addison's nerves calmed, the trio returned to the stage with fresh drinks in hand. Fear and tension dissolved into laughter and delight. Before they knew it, the bartender announced last call.

Addison and Veronica linked arms as they scampered into the parking lot, the spark of laughter still ablaze.

"He's cute," Veronica whispered. "Cuter than Chris."

"You think?" Addison replied as they approached Veronica's black BMW. "I don't know. I think Chris is sexy, just in a different way."

"If you consider dirty hippies sexy," Veronica teased as she climbed into the driver's seat.

"You sure you're okay to drive?" Addison asked, her hand resting on the top of Veronica's open door.

"I promise I am." Veronica smiled. "Bye, babe."

Addison joined Tye, who waved to Veronica as she drove off. "She seems really cool," he said in approval.

Tye drove Addison home, escorting her from the car to the porch. Silence hung in the air. Their eyes locked in a gaze glossed with the edge of a buzz and glistening with the optimism of budding love. Or lust. The porch caressed them in warm light while the street beyond lay cold and empty. Tye's fingers grazed Addison's neck as they slowly slid into her hair. He pulled her close, pressing his warm lips into hers. She tasted citrus on his tongue. There were no hairs tickling her chin, nothing stopping her from pushing deeper into the kiss. Her cheeks burned as his hands moved lower. Midback. Lower back. Hips.

"I better get inside," Addison interrupted, licking her lips as she backed toward the front door.

Tye grinned.

"I had a really good time." She gave him one last hug.

"I did too," he replied, promising to set up another date soon.

Once inside, Addison hurried to the living room, where she peeked through the blinds. The orange Chevy backed out of the driveway and disappeared down the dimly lit street. Addison melted into the couch. It took her a few minutes to recover before going upstairs and getting ready for bed.

Once all the doors were closed and locked and Addison was curled up in her comforter, her phone vibrated, informing her she had received a text. *It must be Tye,* she thought. Did he miss her already? Had he already decided what their next date would be?

UNKNOWN

You missed the real clue

It will be waiting for you

ELEVEN

ADDISON

NOVEMBER 30, 2024

RAINDROPS WEPT from the windshield before being swept away by the slow but steady touch of the wipers. Black clouds stippled the sky, which let out a rumble so wrathful it felt like the car shook. Addison glanced down at her phone screen, where she had Google Maps pulled up, showing she had arrived at 214 W. Caldetto Drive, Redlands, Maine. It was the only 214 W. Caldetto in or around the city; she had made sure of it.

After receiving the latest message from Unknown the night before, Addison had decided it was time to start getting to the bottom of everything. While Unknown had implied she had missed a clue at Rusty Tavern, she thought it best to begin with the clues her patient had left her instead, hopefully throwing Unknown off track in the process. Chris would be discharged tomorrow, and together they could formulate a plan to address Unknown.

GPS had taken her into rural Redlands, down an

unpaved road that wound and weaved through hills and trees for miles. At the end of the road, she was met by a small fishing shack whose deck extended over a small, partially frozen lake. Everything outside the hazy glow of her headlights vanished into darkness as the light of day slipped away, making her second-guess if going here alone was a good idea.

By then, the car windows had almost completely fogged, cuing her exit into the cold drizzle. She pressed her hands deep into her jacket pockets. Earth crunched beneath her boots. She mounted three weatherworn wooden steps that felt as though they could collapse at any moment. A quick twist of the doorknob—locked. Cupping her hands, she peered into a dirty window beside the door, but it was too dark to see anything. Perhaps this was what the key opened? She ran back to the car to retrieve it from her bag.

When she returned, she tried the key, but it wouldn't fit. If her patient had wanted her to find this place, he must have left a way to get in, she thought. She circled the shack, testing each window along the way, but to no avail. Around back on the deck, almost completely concealed by a mess of fishing net, buoys, and stacked barrels, was another door. Addison struggled to drag everything away, her arms still sore from performing CPR days prior. The door was locked and, unsurprisingly, the key did not fit. At the bottom of the door, she noticed a large dog door.

Dropping down on all fours, Addison contorted her petite body to squeeze through the opening, feeling deep scratches carve themselves into her ribs. Once inside the shack and back on two feet, she used the light of her phone to scan the room for a light switch. With a flick of her finger, light poured into the room.

It was a complete mess. Papers were scattered every-where—on the floor, on a plaid couch, and on work-benches that lined the walls. As she walked deeper into the room, kicking papers aside, she noticed something. She froze in place before moving anything else.

Follow the yellow brick road. She recalled the words on the cassette tape. Despite the appearance of disarray, the papers were laid out strategically. Some had a subtle yellow marking on the edge. Taking care where she stepped, Addison picked up each paper along the way as they wound her through the room—over a coffee table, past a small twin bed, and into a kitchenette, where the path stopped right beneath a framed painting of a lion lying beside a lamb.

Addison gripped the edges of the wooden frame, expecting to easily remove it, but it was stuck. She tugged and tugged. It must have been glued on. She scanned the room, locating a hammer on one of the workbenches. Tucking the claw end of the hammer under the edge of the frame, she worked to pry it loose, grunting as she applied more force. Soon, it busted free. She caught her footing. The painting crashed to the floor breaking the frame on impact. On the wall, a small cubby had been unveiled. It was filled with stacks of papers among other things.

Addison reached inside and grabbed the first item, a

ticket stub, much of which was too worn to read. What she could make out was the year 1973, and the band, Pink Floyd. Next was what appeared to be the disembodied hard cover of a book. It was thick and weathered. Black mold dotted the pages. Its edges were frayed and mangled.

The cover was mostly black, with silver embossed vinelike designs enveloping the words. In the center it read *Official Handbook of the Darkside of the Rainbow.* Beneath the title were a pair of skulls, also embossed, but in the same faded black color as the cover. Was this the *Darkside* her patient had been referring to?

Next, she pulled out a newspaper clipping, which had another clipping stapled to it.

The Berkeley Spotlight

Franklin Edwards is one of our brightest students, a double major in both music theory and premed with a bachelor's degree in chemical engineering. Edwards says, "My dream is to become the best neurosurgeon in my hometown of Redlands, Maine, and still maintain enough time to play drums and raise a family." Edwards has received an award of distinction and several votes of high praise from faculty.

Berkeley Badger

March 7, 1976

On the steps of the grand west door of LeConte Hall, Jenny Hartford stumbled upon a scene she could only describe as grisly. What was later confirmed to be a human brain had been cut and mangled to form a triangle. The identity of the victim remains unknown, though many students speculate it belongs to physics major John Finch, who has been missing for two weeks. Local authorities have been notified and are actively working on the case. This comes just months after a heart was found in a bathroom at Bowles Hall. The heart was later confirmed to be of animal origin after thorough investigation by local police. However, tensions have been high with the rise in missing-person cases and now the appearance of mangled organs. As a result, many students have dropped out. Was this the last organ, or will there be more to come?

Beneath the clippings, on a piece of lined paper, was a handwritten note.

The year was 1973. A group of music theory majors at University of Berkeley stumbled upon a discovery that ultimately led to the creation of one of the darkest secret societies to come out of the 1970s. Yet no one but their victims know they exist. And myself, of course. That is why I have begun writing this text and compiling all the evidence I have to finally shed light on this cult. Expose them for who they are. It is time to put an end to Darkside.

Backmasking = the art of listening to music backwards and unveiling secret messages. What began as a night filled with drugs, alcohol, and experimentation led to their discovery and subsequent belief that musicians hid secret messages within their music influenced by a supernatural force or entity. In order to speak to the entity with precision, they utilized a Ouija board.

This group of friends became infatuated with listening to every record they could find in reverse, with their favorites being Pink Floyd, Led Zeppelin, and The Beatles. They even went on to create records of their own that, from what I have read, their Official Handbook of the Darkside of the Rainbow touts as being divinely inspired works. Religious music even. Though I still am not sure exactly what entity they are speaking with.

What started as LSD-induced experimentation quickly transformed into a series of radical crimes that to this day remain unsolved. Whether it be by "divine intervention," as they would call it, or purely skill, they have managed to get by without leaving behind evidence, DNA or otherwise. I suspect their network of influence has played a role in that as well, infiltrating the local police force. These allegations are undeniable and include several horrific murders. I, unfortunately, have been witness to some of these crimes firsthand. Thus, I understand the magnitude of evil that Darkside of the Rainbow *embodies. My connection to the cult places a constraint on my ability to stop them, as I run the risk of harming people I love.*

What I can tell you, dear reader, is that on the night of June 17, 1973, Jane Thatcher and Jack Waterford founded Darkside of the Rainbow after what they describe as a spiritual awakening during the Pink Floyd performance at New York's Saratoga Performing Arts Center on the Dark Side of the Moon tour. They soon recruited Jack's longtime best friend, Paul Stewart, the beauty to Jack's brains of the operation.

The rest of the paper had been torn. Suddenly, Addison heard a car door slam shut. Instinct pulled her toward the ground, where she held her breath. The light switch was too far away to reach in time. Her ears homed in on the sound of footsteps mounting the steps. Her heart thrashed against her chest. There were still so many papers to look through. She scanned the room for something to carry everything in. Just underneath the bed was a leather satchel. Like a soldier, she crawled across the ground. Papers slipped and scraped beneath her forearms. With a grunt, she reached for the satchel and dragged it closer. The doorknob began jiggling forcefully, then a fist pounded against the door. She dumped the contents of the satchel and scooped everything from the cubby inside, securing the bag over her head cross-body-style.

Footsteps hurried, stomping against the wooden deck around the side of the shack. Hands pounded against the siding. Addison ran for the front door. A quick look out the window revealed a black sedan parked next to her car, its headlights still gleaming. No one was in sight. She had begun unlocking the door when glass shattered behind her. A violent swoosh prefaced the spread of flames that engulfed the room by way of the papers. Then a second Molotov cocktail whizzed into the room.

Adrenaline surged through Addison's body as she freed the door from its final lock and tore it open. She burst onto the steps, a cloud of smoke in her wake. Her foot crashed through the last wooden step into the ground beneath as it broke. Thud. Her palms scraped against the ground as she caught her fall, then shook her foot loose. Footsteps raced across the deck. Whoever was there was coming. Fast. Before she stood to her feet, she pulled her keys from her pocket.

"You've got nowhere to go," a man's voice barked.

While running, Addison slipped her fingers through the eyeholes of the cat-knuckles key chain Norah had gifted her. She'd never thought she would have to use them but was now immensely grateful she had them. Even more grateful she had been pressured into latching them onto her keys.

The man lunged from the deck, catching his fall on the dirt. Addison thrust her fist into the wall of his front tire. It hissed as the air escaped. She then thrust the points into the back tire, working to make a wider tear. The knuckles became stuck.

His steps quickened. She tugged harder as he neared the front of the car, almost losing her balance with a final successful jolt. She ran. Just out of his grip she flung her car door open, then closed, smashing the lock button. Her trembling hands found the ignition key and shoved it inside. Just as the engine turned over, the man slammed his hands on the hood of her car, walking them along the A pillar and toward the door handle. Wicked eyes glared at her from behind a ski mask. The engine fired up and she hurled the car into reverse. It didn't matter what was behind her. Rapid breaths dominated her as anxiety gripped tighter. She was beginning to feel light headed.

"Open the door," he spat, punching at the window and clawing at the handle.

The gas pedal hit the floorboard. She fought to control the car as it gunned backward, then whipped back around into drive. The man fell to his knees, blending in with the black of night. Flames raged from the fishing shack, a glow that lingered in Addison's rearview mirror as she sped away. Her hands trembled as she squeezed them tighter around the steering wheel until her knuckles were white. She focused on her breath. Deep inhale. Long exhale.

TWELVE
ADDISON

WHEN ADDISON AWOKE, her comforter was still clenched in her fist. It was a shield, a cloudlike fortress that protected her from being found. Her dresser guarded the locked bedroom door. The chair wouldn't have been strong enough. Was Unknown watching her?

Sunlight glowed through the window, a welcome sight after days of rain and gloom. It caught in the leaves of her plants and exposed the particles of dust that twirled through the air. Looking at her phone, which was clenched tightly in her other hand, she realized she didn't have much time to get ready. She threw on a pair of jeans, slip-on Vans, and a white baby tee. It was her go-to in a time crunch. She brushed her teeth, added the cipher and book into the leather satchel with the rest of the clues her patient had left her, and headed for Community Hospital to pick up Chris. Coffee would have to wait.

A nurse wheeled Chris down to the loading zone at the front of the hospital, where she helped maneuver him into the car. Addison tossed his crutches into the back seat. She and Chris thanked the nurse before shutting their doors. Grinning ear to ear, Chris reached over to hug Addison. His tanned skin was still spattered with yellow-green bruises. His beard had been trimmed short, revealing a strong jaw that Addison hadn't ever seen. Butterflies danced in her stomach.

"What have I missed?" Chris asked as Addison put the car into drive.

Addison released a gust of air. "Where do I even begin?"

It took her the entire twenty-minute drive to his apartment to explain all the new revelations she'd come across. For ten of the twenty, he berated her for going to the fishing shack alone.

Once they arrived, she pulled the leather bag full of her patient's clues from the floor of the back seat and rested it on her lap.

"I still need to finish going through everything," she said.

"Let me help you." Chris reached over and held her hand. She had missed the feeling of his rough, calloused palm.

The car idled in guest parking. Addison hesitated to respond at first. "I don't know, I really don't want to drag you into this."

"I'm already invested." He looked down at his cast.

"I thought you said you thought it was just a coincidence," Addison fumed.

"Well, I thought it was at first, until you told me about the black sedan that followed you to that shack. What if it was the same guy? Addison, please let me help you."

Addison liked the idea of having Chris's help. He made her feel safe. She knew that even with a broken leg, he was capable of protecting her.

"Okay, you can help, but please be careful." Addison tensed. "You only have one good leg."

Chris smirked, revealing a deepest dimple in his right cheek that had been previously hidden. "You too. Whatever is going on seems to be pretty serious, and we can't take any chances." He inhaled deeply. "If anything happens to you . . . if anyone hurts you . . . I-I will kill them without hesitation."

Addison's heart skipped a beat. His determination to keep her safe was alluring. And, while she didn't want to put him in danger—or worse, in a position to kill someone —she knew it was no longer safe to get to the bottom of this alone.

"I think you should hold on to this for now." Addison handed him the bag. He pulled the strap over his head to secure it. "It will be safer with you," she said. "Maybe you can start looking for more clues."

He nodded in agreement. "There's something else I've been meaning to tell you. While I was in the hospital, I couldn't stop thinking about that nurse you told me about that was coding your patient with you. Jack. Something doesn't sit right with me about that story. I even asked some of my nurses what they thought, and they agreed that it sounds like he was being negligent. Can you go back to the hospital and talk to him?"

Her lip curled upward in disgust. "I am not going back there."

He shrugged. "Just a thought."

"I meant to send an email to my manager to file a complaint, but I got wrapped up in all of this Darkside stuff."

"Will you be able to get his contact information if you file a complaint?" Chris asked.

Addison tilted her head. "No, probably not. I guess I could just call Harlow and say I have something of Jack's to return."

"I think that would be best; that way you can actually have a chance to track him down," Chris said. "Are you coming up?"

"I actually have to stop by Rusty Tavern while I'm on this side of town." Addison said. "But I will walk you upstairs."

At his doorway, she promised to be careful. Chris leaned over and gave Addison a gentle peck on the lips. Even his quick kisses were good.

"Keep your doors locked, just in case," Addison warned as she walked away.

"Yes, ma'am," he said.

Back in the car, Addison called Harlow, her manager at Jefferson Memorial, who answered after three short rings. After working with her for over five years, Addison knew just how to convince Harlow that she needed Jack's number.

"I don't know if it's appropriate to give out that information, Addison," Harlow said.

"I understand, but I have something of his that I need to return," Addison lied. "If you lost something important, wouldn't you want the person who found it to have your contact information?"

A beat. "I don't have it easily accessible."

"If you could at least tell me his last name, I could find him on Facebook or something."

Addison could hear Harlow shifting through papers. "Here it is. Waterford."

Addison barely managed to write down the number Harlow provided as her jaw collapsed. *Jack Waterford.* The cofounder of Darkside of the Rainbow. She steadied her breath, unsure if it was anger or panic welling up inside her. Graciously, Addison hung up, her heart picking up speed, and dialed Jack's number.

"Hi, you've reached Jack, leave a message and I'll get back to you . . ." *Beep.*

Click.

Not wanting him to know it was her, she avoided leaving a message. Perhaps this way he would see the missed call and call her back. Then she'd have an opportunity to lay into him. To question him.

She sat in her surprise for a moment before texting Chris.

CHRIS

No freaking way!

THIRTEEN

HANNAH

OCTOBER 31, 1976

HANNAH AND CARRIE were each other's alibi Halloween night. Carrie chose to spend her night with Rodney at a prestigious frat house party oozing with jocks and prom queens. Together they were the quintessential extract of popularity. They wore an *I Dream of Jeannie* couple's costume. Carrie's Coke-bottle figure was draped in pink-and-red flowing fabric, her midriff bare; Rodney's broad shoulders boasted confidence in his tailored blue Major Nelson suit—a timeless couple that Hannah was sure would go on to be married and successful. People would gush about Rodney's profound impact on society, Carrie's philanthropic achievements, and the way their children were the spitting image of their stunning parents.

Hannah's hand slipped from Carrie's as they parted ways in the dormitory hall. She ducked underneath Paul's outstretched arm and into his apartment, where some of his friends had already become comfortable on the couch.

"You remember my friends," Paul said as he shut the door.

Hannah flashed her palm—a quick hi—then folded her arms.

"This is Jane." Paul pointed to the naturally beautiful blonde who had once pressed a dagger to Hannah's throat. Hannah's breath hiccupped. Warmth illuminated Jane's face from her radiant smile. She was sugar and ice.

"Jack."

An average-looking man with thin lips and a mustache leaned toward Hannah from the couch to shake her hand. He struck her as analytical. The kind of guy who could solve an impossible mathematical equation with nothing more than his mind. Pedantic, diffident socially, but aware of what was expected.

"Yessenia."

The Hispanic woman with a gentle smile and thick, peaked eyebrows tugged her shirt down, then hugged Hannah.

"You can sit here." Yessenia offered her spot on the couch right between Jack and Jane. Hannah paused for a few heartbeats, then shimmied into the couch. The spot warmed her thighs.

Paul had cleaned up his apartment some. The only beer bottles around were the ones being drunk. Explicit magazines had been tucked away somewhere and the ashtray cleaned. He had made a small attempt to decorate for Halloween. Black and orange streamers. Stray pumpkins.

An album was playing that Hannah didn't recognize, but it was in the vein of Pink Floyd and Fleetwood Mac. A multilayered sound. It evoked emotion—nostalgia, euphoria, even sadness. The particular song that played had breathtaking harmonies, dominating guitar riffs, and whimsical charm. A "Rhiannon"-like essence.

Verse 1:
In the shadows of the moonlit sky
A whisper calls my name
A voice that lingers like a sigh
It guides me through the endless game
By the echoes of a distant dream
I find a door I've never seen
I step inside to free my mind
Embrace the life I've left behind

Chorus:
Possession, it takes me high
Opens up my mind and soul so wide
Unraveling the mystery
Of love, of life, of you and me

"What band is this?" Hannah inquired.

"Do you like it?" Jane asked with an open posture as she leaned nearer to Hannah. The woman who had salivated at the hope of tasting Hannah's blood nights earlier was cozying up to her like they'd were longtime friends.

Kindred spirits. There was no trace of malice in her eyes, only unbridled sincerity and kindness.

"It's really good."

"That's us," Paul said.

"Seriously?" Hannah's mouth slackened. Though the voice sounded familiar, she hadn't realized Paul could sing. Especially that well.

"This is just a demo of our first album, still pretty raw," Jack interjected, his voice monotonous. "I'm still working on post-production edits and mastering."

"There's room for another musician," Jane honeyed. "Do you play any instruments, Hannah?"

"N-no," she stuttered. "But I've always wanted to."

Jane twirled a piece of Hannah's hair through her fingers. "I'll think of something for you to play."

"We need to focus," Jack redirected, shifting on the couch. "It's already dark out, and we haven't gone over the instructions yet."

Hannah's eyes flared with panic as she looked to Paul. Somehow he felt safe, but she knew he was just as dangerous as the others.

"Jack is right," Paul said, sitting on the edge of the coffee table to face Hannah. "Tonight is a big night for you, Hannah."

She gulped. Paul pulled Hannah's hand from beneath her leg and stroked her palm, pulling it onto his lap. Jane continued to play with Hannah's hair. Her body felt numb.

"Tonight, the veil between worlds is at its thinnest," Paul said.

"Between worlds?" Hannah stared blankly.

"Ours and the spirit realm," he explained.

"Which is why"—Jack leaned forward, using his hands to talk—"it's the perfect night for your first kill. Bigger payout. Better rewards."

"But . . ." Hannah's eyes locked on to Paul's. "I already did my first kill."

"Human kill," Jane said with enthusiasm as she began braiding Hannah's hair.

"I don't know." Hannah's stomach churned. "What's in it for me?"

"Tell me, Hannah, when you went home yesterday, did you receive what you set your mind to receive?" Paul asked.

"Well, yes, but . . ."

"Now imagine how much more you can be rewarded with, especially on a night like this, if you align yourself with receiving and offer something as valuable as a human life. The possibilities are endless."

"But who am I offering it to?"

They all looked at each other.

"Aamon," Jane whispered.

"A very powerful entity," Jack interjected, "but we will go over all of that later, once you have proven yourself."

"What do you say?" Paul gripped her hand tighter. The warmth of his thigh permeated the back of her hand.

"I-I don't know." Hannah felt sweat forming under her breasts.

"I told you this was a bad idea." Jack stormed into the kitchen.

"Come on, Jack, relax." Yessenia chased after him. Their indiscernible whispers echoed from the kitchen.

Jane tilted her head back in Jack's direction. "He never lies, Jack. If he said she is chosen, she is chosen."

"Have a little faith, brother." Paul's grip on Hannah's hand weakened for a moment. He seemed unable to multitask.

"I just don't even know how I would do it." Hannah's voice reeled Paul's attention back in.

"I'll teach you." He smiled. "Wait here."

When he returned, he had a sheet of LSD. It was different than the one they had taken previously. Sitting in front of Hannah, he clipped off a small square with an image of a strawberry on it. With a delicate hand, he placed the paper on the tip of his tongue, then pulled Hannah onto his lap for a kiss. He grazed his tongue over hers, sharing the LSD as it dissolved. As she pulled away, her lip caught in his teeth. One more possessive kiss lingered on her lips before she was fully released from his grasp. Heat erupted through her body, blossoming into a craving for something beyond kissing. Hannah knew exactly how to make it happen.

"Rule number one." A renewed Jack returned to the couch with an ice-cold beer. "Do exactly as we say."

Hannah nodded.

"Rule number two: Your mind must always focus on receiving both what *he* wants to tell you or show you as well as what you desire. That means you can't think about being scared or let your mind wander onto other things. Power thrives in a focused mind. Distraction is the impuissance of the powerless." Jack took a swig of his beer, then continued. "There are limits to what you can receive, though *his* gifts abound."

"Jack, just get to the point," Jane said.

"We've already done some preliminary communications and preparations, but you must speak with *him* in order to know exactly who your target is."

Paul cleared off the coffee table, where Yessenia placed an Ouija board. While she set everything up and provided Hannah a brief overview of the board, Paul chose a Beatles album to play. "Come Together" began playing in reverse, a menacing melody sweeping through the speakers.

Yessenia guided Hannah's hands onto the planchette and offered a nod of encouragement. Hannah couldn't help but wonder how such a kind and seemingly innocent person had become involved in such a dangerous cult. A tu quoque argument indeed.

Hannah cleared her mind as instructed and focused on receiving. What? She didn't know. The music permeated her ears, a palate cleanser to her thoughts.

"I come to you, open to receive," Hannah began. "Tell me what you want me to do."

A potent feeling washed over her. Something supernatural. A surge of confidence powered through her. Capability. Just when she was about to lift her hands from the planchette, it began to move. She wasn't moving it, but there were no other hands on it but her own. It began to spell.

T-W-O C-A-S-P-E-R-S Y-O-U A-R-E O-N-E
T-I-M-E T-O R-U-I-N S-A-M-M-Y-S F-U-N

"Do you want me to kill Sammy?" Hannah asked.

YES

"Is Sammy a boy or a girl?"

G-I-R-L

"Will she be dressed as Casper?"

NO

"Is the person she's with dressed as Casper?"

YES

R-E-P-L-A-C-E

"What will Sammy be dressed up as?"

W-O-N-D-E-R W-O-M-A-N

"How will I find her?"

R-E-C-E-I-V-E

Hannah took a deep breath and cleared her mind, pressing out every thought until even the sound of the music disappeared from her perception. A voice popped into her mind; it was her own, but she wasn't in control of it. *Cedar and Euclid, 9:13.* Hannah looked for a clock.

"What time is it?"

"Eight fifty." Jack peered at his watch.

"We have to hurry," Hannah said.

The group looked to each other conspiratorially.

"What did he tell you?" Paul asked.

"Cedar and Euclid at nine thirteen. I have to dress up as Casper."

"Here." Jack tossed a folded-up paper bag to Hannah. Inside were a white outfit and a Casper mask.

"How'd you know?"

"Remember the part about preliminary communications?" Jack said flatly.

Paul drove while the rest of the group stayed back at the apartment. At exactly 9:10, he and Hannah arrived at Cedar and Euclid. Paul parked his Firebird right around the corner, leaving just enough time for a quick pep talk. Hannah hesitated to get out. Paul encouraged her, enticing with the implication of something more than a kiss. She adjusted the mask at 9:12 and exited the car.

The air smelled like Halloween—cold, fresh, and distinctly autumn. Fallen maple leaves collected in the gutters. Kids and teenagers alike crowded the sidewalks and scurried across the street, clutching their buckets tight. Their voices and actions boasted of a confidence that could only come from the mystique of a costume.

At 9:13, Casper and Wonder Woman mounted the curb. Sammy. She was tall and young but couldn't have been younger than seventeen, yet Hannah had never met her. Hannah observed her. She moved loosely, her arms flailing while she talked and talked. Her friendly ghost companion was silent and stiff. Whoever was under that mask looked to be about five foot seven and 135 pounds, just like Hannah.

"Let's go to the Ashfords'; they have the best candy," the girl dressed as Casper said.

"I can't go there," Sammy said. "If they see me drunk, they'll tell my parents. You go. Get me something good!"

"Your parents won't care," Casper said. "Whatever, I'll be right back. Stay here."

Sammy nodded and started spinning in circles. On the third spin she stumbled, but caught her balance. Casper disappeared into the house, welcomed in for a cup of hot chocolate by a couple so picture perfect it could have been Carrie and Rodney from the future. This was Hannah's chance.

Hannah ran over to Sammy and locked arms with her, angling their path toward Paul's park car. Her stomach twisted and turned, but she kept performing. Kept her eye on the prize.

"Where are we going?" Sammy giggled, gripping Hannah's arm tight.

Hannah didn't reply. They rounded the corner and entered an alley that ran behind the houses. It was dimly lit and littered in trash that hadn't quite made it into the garbage truck during pickup. The Firebird's engine was running, but Paul was leaning against the front fender.

"Ooh, you're cute," Sammy slurred, tripping over her own feet.

Paul caught her and pressed a chloroform-soaked cloth to her face. She struggled. He pressed harder. As she grew limp, he tossed the rag to the ground and dragged her into the back seat, where Hannah had already opened the door. Both doors slammed in unison, and they sped away undetected.

FOURTEEN
ADDISON

ADDISON DROVE to the Rusty Tavern, ready to search for the clue she had supposedly missed. The ambience of the bar was much different during the day. Instead of the edgy dive bar facade it had taken on the night of the concert, it had transformed back into a dirty hole-in-the-wall. Like Cinderella's carriage, it was a pumpkin again. Hardly anybody was there except for a few overweight men with greasy, slicked-back hair and suspenders. Addison's entrance garnered their attention, their heads turning and tracking her as she made her way through the arches and into the bathroom.

Unsure of what she could have missed, she began her search in the stall where she had found the message her annoying friend had left. The thought of it still bothered her. There was nothing out of the ordinary. Nothing in the little metal trash canister. Nothing in the toilet tank. Even the other two stalls were clueless, just like her.

Unless . . .

Returning to the middle stall, she searched the scratches on the walls for any hidden messages.

Jessica 🤍 *Hugh*
Bite Me

The only other legible carvings on the walls were curse words and a large phallic symbol. Turning around, she noticed a marking on the door of the stall. In an effort to expose it to light, she closed the door, revealing a triangle prism with a line passing from one side to the other, where it emerged as a rainbow. Exactly like the Dark Side of the Moon album cover. Addison snapped a picture on her phone.

Is this the clue? she thought, letting the door of the stall slam shut behind her. It certainly wasn't revelatory. *Ping.*

UNKNOWN

Close, but that's not it.

Her shoulders hunched, and she could feel panic flare in her eyes. Reflexively, she ducked into a stall and slid the lock shut. Eyes squeezed tight, she gulped and began to regulate her breathing. How had Unknown seen her? Her mind raced. *Are there cameras? There must be cameras somewhere.*

Scraping up every ounce of bravery she could find, Addison searched the bathroom. If there were any cameras, they were well hidden.

Above the sinks was a mirror that spanned the length

of the wall. Remembering a video she'd seen about two-way mirrors, she placed her finger against the glass. If there was a gap between her finger and the reflection, then it was a real mirror. No gap meant it was a two-way mirror.

There was no gap.

At this point, her heart was hammering against her chest, but she knew she was being watched. Not wanting to look scared, she took extra care to fake a calm, cool, and collected demeanor. It wasn't hard. She'd done it a thousand times as a nurse, forced to mask her defeat and tears with a brave face. Without this skill, she would have certainly broken down in those fragile moments after an unsuccessful code blue, or after offering a brave apology to the screaming mother who had just lost her son. This was another moment when Addison's tears and fears would have to wait for another time.

There was still a clue to be found. Delicate footsteps led her along the row of sinks. *Ping.*

UNKNOWN

Warmer.

She continued on her path until she reached the window. *Ping.*

UNKNOWN

Ding, ding, ding. We have a winner.

On the windowsill was a small heart-shaped box. It had been crafted from some sort of dark wood. Examining it closer, she saw the letters *JT* etched into the lid. With some force, she pried it open. Inside was a fortune cookie paper. On one side were the numbers *1, 0, 1, 9, 7, 6.* The other side a quote:

A HEART IS NOT JUDGED BY HOW MUCH YOU LOVE; BUT BY HOW MUCH YOU ARE LOVED BY OTHERS.

Once the paper was tucked back inside and the lid secured, Addison threw up her hands.

"What the hell does this even mean?" she demanded aloud. Texting seemed pointless if they were already watching her. "Hello," she shouted. Her voice echoed.

When she realized she wasn't going to get a response, she snatched the box and tucked it into her front pocket. She pushed into the last stall, where she had remembered the toilet seat was barely hanging on. It didn't take much effort for her to shimmy it free. With the heavy seat in her hands, she bolted for the mirror and smashed the seat against it. Reeling back with all of her strength, she swung at the mirror again. And again. Glass shattered. Shielding her face with her arm, she ducked away from the shards. The toilet seat tumbled through the mirror to the other side.

The room behind the mirror was dark and small—a storage room with very few items stored in it. A shadowy figure ran out of Addison's view before she could really see who it was. She ran for the bathroom door. Glass crunched and slipped beneath her feet. Just as she reached the door, ready to rip it open, she slipped and fell. A piece of glass dug into her shin. Wincing, she ripped it out and scrambled back to her feet, tearing the door open. Blood began slowly saturating her jeans.

Her eyes kept scanning for anything out of the ordinary and anyone suspicious. Past the archways, her gaze snagged on someone running out of the bar. The rusty screen door trembled shut in their wake. Though she'd only caught a glimpse, it was long enough to see that whoever it was was wearing a black hoodie pulled over their head and black sweatpants. Could it be the same person she'd encountered at the fish shack? It was hard to tell for sure, but this person seemed more petite. Addison pulled out her phone.

ADDISON

Who are you.

A beat.

UNKNOWN

In due time.

Talk to the bartender

Metal screeched against the floor as Addison pulled a barstool out. Realizing her cut was a little deeper than she'd originally thought, she grabbed a wad of cocktail napkins and applied pressure.

"One shot of tequila, please," Addison requested. "And some more napkins." She needed something to calm her nerves.

The bartender nodded to confirm, then poured her a shot. Before he could turn around, she had downed it.

"Are you Addison?" he inquired, both hands resting on the bar top. She met his question with a judgmental gaze.

"Who wants to know?" she inquired, pressing a fresh clump of napkins to her shin.

"I take that as a yes," he said as he slid an envelope to her.

Reluctantly, she opened the letter to find a piece of paper with magazine cut-out letters.

**LEAVE ThE KEY
AT ThE bAR.**

Whoever Unknown was, they knew about the key. Were they watching her even more closely than she thought? Were they watching her inside her house?

Panic welled up inside her all over again. She ordered another shot. Her body shuddered at the bite of the tequila.

"Who left this? What did they look like?" Addison clamored for answers.

"Didn't really get a good look, sorry," the bartender replied as he dried a glass.

"Okay, but you must have seen them long enough for them to tell you to give this to me. You must've seen what they were wearing. Was it a man or a woman?"

"Look, lady, I'm not a detective. I don't remember." His eyes remained on the glass he was drying.

"Was it that woman that just left before I sat down?" Addison pleaded for more information.

"I didn't see any woman leave," he said, pausing a little too long while he put the glass away. "It was left here the other night."

"The night that Releanor Igby played?" Addison questioned, her eyes now burning a hole right through him.

"Yes." He finally looked at her. "And they said if you didn't get it that night, you'd be back in a couple of days."

"How did you know to give it to me?"

He looked toward the other patrons. "Have you seen what the regular customers look like?"

Without another word, she paid for her tab, leaving a sizable tip on account of the blood and broken mirror. While he ran her card, she ran through her options. If she left the key, all of this would be over: Unknown would stop messaging her, they'd stop harassing her, and no one else would get hurt.

Images of her patient flashed in her mind. Trauma from her inability to save him tugged at her heart. For some reason, he'd fought hard to get to Addison and leave her clues to finish what he'd started. If she left the key, all of his hard work would have been for nothing. His death would have been for nothing. As tough as it was, she decided to maintain her loyalty to her patient and keep the key. If anyone was going to find out what the key opened, she was determined it would be her.

Back in the cold winter air, she hurried to her car and fired up the engine along with the heater. She rubbed her hands together for warmth before pulling out of the driveway.

Like a vigilante, she felt her eyes searching for stalkers, jumping from the windows to the rearview mirror, determined not to miss anything. As she turned onto the highway, a car appeared in her rearview mirror. A black sedan. At first Addison thought nothing of it—until it sped within feet of her and she realized it was *the* black sedan.

Rage sparked inside her. But her rage quickly turned to terror when the car started tapping her bumper. Her body was thrust forward. Another violent tap. They were taunting her.

Her foot dug deep into the gas pedal, and the speedometer climbed—80, 85, 90, 100, 110—her panic concealed only by the concentration it took not to crash as she approached a bend. In that moment, she wished she hadn't taken those tequila shots. The black sedan picked up speed, angling toward her back fender, ready to pounce. If the driver was successful, they both would surely die.

As they rounded the bend, a semi truck appeared from the other direction. Unable to correct in time, the black sedan clipped the side of the semi. Addison pressed the brake as safely as she could as she watched a mess of metal and fire unfold behind her. There wasn't any doubt in her mind that whoever was chasing her could not survive that crash.

A scream erupted from her mouth as tears welled in her eyes. Should she stop? Maybe she could help, or at the very least confirm who had been following her. Then she realized that not only had she been drinking, but she was speeding. Another crime that could jeopardize her nursing license. Reluctance choked her. It went against everything she believed in to forgo helping the injured. She continued driving.

FIFTEEN

ADDISON

Addison's drive home matched the speed limit at most. After what she had just experienced, she couldn't take any chances, even if she wanted to. Her hands trembled as she called Chris. Every mirror in her car was subject to the scrutiny of her cobalt eyes. Always scanning. Ready to catch anything out of the ordinary.

"Addy the Baddy," Chris sang as he picked up the phone.

Addison's voice hiccupped, unable to hold back the tears she had just holstered.

"What's wrong?" His voice was full of concern.

Addison explained what she could through jumpy breaths.

"Can I please come over?" she sniffled.

"Of course you can," Chris replied. "Do you want me to come get you?"

"No, I'm just going to grab a few things at home real

quick, then I'll head over. I'm pulling into my driveway now."

"Please be careful," he insisted.

Gravel crunched beneath her tires as they rolled to a stop. Overcast skies threatened to rain, adding to the ominous energy that pulsed through Addison's body. An overwhelming urge to look around and look behind came over her, but she fought it. Deep breaths. Once inside her house, she shut the door behind her and twisted the dead bolt.

Skipping multiple steps, she ran upstairs and into her room. Hangers hit the floor as she grabbed a large tote bag from the closet and began shoveling clothes and necessities inside. In a panic, she hoisted up the mattress, plunging a searching hand inside. Her fingers felt nothing but box springs and cloth. A sigh of relief escaped her when she remembered everything was in the satchel at Chris's apartment.

Returning to the hallway, she took a moment to collect herself. The door to her parents' room was closed. Had she closed it? Her stomach sank. It was possible, though she couldn't remember shutting it. Holding her breath, she extended her hand and gently wrapped each finger around the door handle, ready to open the door back up to its usual half-open position. Suddenly, something fell, crashing to the floor. Glass shattered. Feet shuffled inside. Addison heard the scuffle of her parents' dresser shifting over the carpet. She retracted her hand and slowly stepped backward, her heart thrashing against her chest. Someone was in the house.

Her pace quickened into a jog as she descended the stairs. The door to her parents' room crashed open. Addison struggled to unlock the front door, mad at herself for locking it. Footsteps pounded on the stairs. She flung the front door open, then slammed it behind her. She ran to her car faster than she had ever run in her life. Eyes glued to the front door, she anticipated seeing whoever was in her house emerge any second. Her left hand smashed the lock button in as she cranked the engine with her right. *How can this be happening again?* Swallowing a dry lump in her throat, she put the car in reverse and crept out of the driveway. Still watching. Hoping to catch someone.

No one emerged.

Ignoring as many stop signs as she safely could, she raced over to Chris's apartment. Maybe it was all in her imagination. Something could have fallen on its own. There was a high probability she had closed the door after examining the photograph of her father. Trauma from witnessing such a horrific car accident—and being chased, for that matter—had likely contributed to her overreaction. But the footsteps heavy on the stairs kept replaying in her mind.

In need of reassurance, she called Veronica on speakerphone. It went straight to voicemail.

"Ronnie, someone was chasing me, and I think they are dead now. Then I came home and I am almost certain someone was in the house," Addison rambled. "Please call me as soon as you get a chance. I'm on my way to Chris's now."

A minute later, a text came through.

VERONICA

OMG Babe! That's terrifying. You need to call the police!! I'm stuck with a client right now, but I'll call as soon as I can.

ADDISON

I can't call the police . . .

I promise I'm safe for now at his place. I just gotta clear my head and figure this out.

VERONICA

sigh okay, well I'm glad you're with him. And you know you can come stay with me anytime if you aren't comfortable staying there.

Be extra careful, luv u

Addison's heart rate slowed as she regulated her breathing.

Chris hobbled to the parking lot with his crutches, ready to receive Addison in his arms. She nuzzled into his warm chest. He squeezed her tighter than he ever had before. Finally, she felt safe, like she could breathe. Even more so once they were locked inside his apartment. Inside a complex that was gated, surveilled, and patrolled.

His place was small. One bedroom, one bathroom. Three surfboards, all well ridden, hung on the living room wall. A Bob Marley "One Love" tapestry was stretched along the otherwise white wall behind his flat-screen TV. A generic metal TV stand housed several gaming consoles and an assortment of Funko Pops. Admittedly, it had come a long way since the first time she had been there, when the living room furniture consisted of a beanbag and unpacked boxes. To Addison's pleasure, Chris had followed the links she'd sent him and purchased a beautiful leather sectional and round walnut coffee table. Lightly used, of course.

"You can put your stuff in the bedroom," he said, pointing with the tip of his crutch.

When Addison returned to the big open space that was the kitchen and living room, the smell of seasoned ground beef and jalapeños greeted her. Chris had prepared tacos for them. Everything was laid out in Tupperware and paper plates on the counter, including onions and finely chopped cilantro. Though it smelled delicious, she was still too shaken up to eat. Later on, she would force herself to take a few bites out of courtesy.

"I think I know what you need," Chris said, tossing his weed pen to her.

She smiled, taking a small inhale. Just enough to help her relax but still maintain mental clarity. Addison nestled into her spot in the corner of the sectional where both long ends met. Chris tossed a black throw blanket over her legs before cozying up next to her.

"Have you had a chance to look through the bag?" Addison inquired. She dug her toes into the crack between the cushions.

"Actually, I have." Chris smiled before sinking his teeth into an overfilled taco.

Addison straightened up.

"Anything earth shattering?"

"Well, sort of." Reaching toward the coffee table, Chris retrieved a slip of paper from among the dumped contents of the leather satchel and offered it to Addison. She snatched up the handwritten note.

When Hannah Garver was 15, she was almost killed by Darkside of the Rainbow. October of 1976, she was lured to the stage of Hearst Greek Theatre at UC Berkeley by her drug dealer. He took advantage of her insecurities and her interest in him. While drugged, the cult performed one of their signature rituals with candles, backwards music, and a Ouija board. Jane, probably the most evil of the entire group simply based on her ability to be just as sweet as she could be sour (a sociopath indeed), pressed a knife to Hannah's throat, drooling at the promise of tasting her blood and the reward she would receive. But to everyone's surprise, the entity they communicated with claimed Hannah was "chosen." Despite this, she was left in the auditorium disheveled and alone with a triangle smudged onto her forehead. Branding her. Her life was spared at a great cost. That is difficult to admit, but her vulnerability at that time made her a perfect candidate to be groomed to become arguably the greatest receiver Darkside ever recruited.

Addison was speechless.

"Are you okay?" Chris asked, wiping his hand with a paper towel before placing it on her shoulder.

"My mom was in this . . . *cult*? I-I have so many questions," Addison couldn't move. Her body went numb. She didn't even know what to feel. Angry? Sad? Scared?

"My jaw literally hit the floor when I read Hannah Garver," Chris said as he shuffled through the papers on the coffee table in search of something else. Their mothers shared a first name and a proclivity for drinking, something they'd bonded over early on. Hannah Cromwell, however, made drinking look sophisticated and chic, the pastime of a world traveler in search of the best surf, the best seafood, and the best self. To her 450,000 followers, she was an inspiration, but to Chris, she was broken.

"I had no idea my mom ever even lived in California. How could she even be involved in something like this?" Addison worked to remember anything from her past that could help her make sense of it.

"This could be what led her to becoming an alcoholic," Chris offered.

Addison nodded in agreement, her gaze vacant.

"Well, this for sure connects her to my patient somehow. It connects me," she said, looking at Chris. "The problem is I'm even more confused now."

"Take a look at this letter," he said.

Dearest Hannah,
As you know, Jack and I were thrilled when

you joined us. You were, after all, the chosen one. Our divine chose to spare your life, and for that we have always held you to a higher standard. You were special. You always had a way of receiving the obscure messages. Your findings have led to an abundance of rewards and wealth, and for that I will forever be grateful. However, your drinking has become a problem. Rarely are you not drunk. Your fighting and drinking has diminished your ability to receive, which has cost us a great deal. When you brought Andrew into our lives, you assured us he would join. You promised he would be an asset. He played guitar. We had tragically just lost Paul and were in need of a new guitarist in order to continue to create our own music. Unfortunately, you were wrong about Andrew. He has disrupted some of our most vital rituals and has made it clear he will not join us. Thus, he must be disposed of. You must get rid of Andrew by any means necessary if you want to maintain your title of Grand Magistrate. I will need proof of his disposal.

Yours supremely,

Jane

"My dad knew about this?" Addison squeezed the letter tighter.

Chris offered a consoling hand.

"Do you think," Addison began, afraid to even say the

words she was thinking. "Could she have killed him? What if he didn't leave us? What if Darkside killed him?"

"At this point, I think anything is possible," Chris admitted.

Addison gritted her teeth. "What else did you find?"

"This." Chris handed her a tattered black-and-white photo that appeared to have been torn from a yearbook. A group of young adults posed with various musical instruments. The picture was titled *Oz Music Club*, with their names listed below: *Amy Brighton, George Crest, Franklin Edwards, Hannah Garver, Paul Stewart, Yessenia Velasquez, Jack Waterford.* The photo was pretty damaged, but Addison could recognize her mom, Hannah, and could see the resemblance to the nurse Jack, though he was much thinner.

"You think all of these people were members of the cult?" Chris asked.

"Probably. We know for sure Paul and Jack were . . . and my mom." Hannah was holding a tambourine in the photo. Her hair was dark, long, and straight, just like Addison remembered. Her skin was clear and her beauty radiant. She wore knee-high boots and a short floral print dress hinting at her feminine figure—perky breasts, a thin waist, and toned legs. Together, the group resembled a popular seventies band like Jefferson Airplane or Fleetwood Mac.

"I need answers," Addison announced, reaching for her phone, "Jack needs to start explaining everything. I've given him more than enough time to call me back on his own, but I can't wait any longer. I don't care if he knows it's me calling." Tapping on the phone icon, she dialed his number and put it on speaker.

Six rings and a click preceded a soft, subdued "Hello?"

It was a female voice.

"Hi, um, is Jack there?" Addison asked.

The woman's voice trembled. "Jack." She paused and began sobbing. "Jack is dead."

Addison's eyes widened. "I-I'm so sorry. Can I ask what happened?"

"A car accident," the woman said, her sobs growing more turbulent.

Even with her mind clamoring for words, Addison was left speechless.

"Who is this?" the woman asked. "How do you know my husband?"

Addison quickly hung up and stared off into space. Like a cow in a thunderstorm, she was vulnerable and scared, yet unable to move.

SIXTEEN

HANNAH

Paul drove a few blocks away from where they had captured Sammy and into a secluded neighborhood. She was still out, slumped over Hannah in the back seat. The street was dark. Several streetlamps had burned out. There were only a couple of trick-or-treaters making their way from door to door.

Halfway down the block, they approached a brown ranch-style home with an attached garage. The porch light was off to deter trick-or-treaters, and the front yard was heavily shaded by a large oak tree. Headlights illuminated the rising garage door as Paul pulled into the driveway, past a parked patrol car, and into the garage.

"What are you doing?" Hannah panicked. "There's a cop here?"

"Relax, it's my brother's house."

"Your brother is a cop?"

"Not just any cop; he's the police chief." Paul put the

car in park and waited for the garage door to close before making his next move.

"But"—Hannah tagged along behind him as he pulled Sammy out of the back seat—"does he know about . . . ?"

"About Darkside of the Rainbow?" The girl was limp in his arms, which flexed as he shifted her weight into a better position.

Hannah nodded.

"Of course he knows. How do you think he became police chief at such a young age? Get the door for me."

Hannah opened the door, and they entered the house through the kitchen. All the blinds were closed, and they were greeted by a stocky man who couldn't have been more than twenty-five years old. There was an obvious resemblance to Paul, though he wasn't as striking. His golden-brown hair was short and his skin weathered and slightly burnt by the sun. His nose was bigger than his brother's and turned down.

He helped Paul lug Sammy into a back bedroom that had been covered in clear plastic. A flat metal autopsy bed had been set up in the center of the otherwise empty room. Sammy's eyes began to flutter open. Her head tossed side to side.

"Go to sleep, sweetie," Paul's brother said, his voice deep and scratchy. He pressed a needle into Sammy's arm, and she drifted back to sleep. Together they secured her wrists to the table and slapped a piece of duct tape over her mouth. Both brothers let out a synchronized sigh, then approached Hannah for a proper introduction.

"You must be Hannah. I'm Greg." He wiped his hand against his jeans before shaking hers. He was wearing a Berkeley PD T-shirt and gray sweatpants.

"Nice to meet you," she said, jarred by his firm handshake.

"I hear it's a big night for you, huh?"

"Apparently it is." Hannah nodded. looking in Paul's direction.

"Well, bro, you ready to begin?" Greg disappeared into a nearby room for a moment, then returned with a spiral-bound notebook. *Official Handbook of the Darkside of the Rainbow* was written on the cover in permanent ink.

Greg flipped through the first few pages, then turned the notebook over to Hannah. "Here, look this over, then we can begin."

First Kill

1. *Link hands with the victim and receive the song*
2. *Light the candles*
3. *Play it in reverse*
4. *Receive the message*
5. *Chant the message*
6. *Set your mind on your desire*
7. *Kill*

Hannah held her victim's limp hand in her right and Paul's in her left. With her deep exhale, the lights flickered and a song began playing in her head. Once she recognized the tune, she told the boys what to play. While they unsheathed the record from its sleeve, Hannah lit the candles that lined the perimeter of the room. The speakers crackled to life as the chaotic sounds of "Revolution 9" played in reverse. The trio began circling the victim as Hannah cleared her mind, ready to receive.

"Turn me on, dead man," she chanted.

The lights flickered as they circled the room. Their faces glowed in the candlelight.

"Turn me on, dead man," the others continued while Hannah focused her mind on receiving what she desired. All of the fear and anxiety fled from her body as quickly as the image of Paul rushed in, deluging her being. His flowing hair. His strong arms. His soft lips. She wanted to be his girlfriend more than anything. Her hands squeezed tight around the handle of a knife that had been resting beside Sammy. The edges were serrated and the handle thick. The lights went black as she positioned the blade directly above the victim's heart. Seconds before the song ended, Hannah plunged the blade deep into Sammy's chest, then pulled it back out. Blood gushed and squirted. After another penetration, crimson pooled on the table beneath.

When the music stopped, the lights came back on. Hannah felt different. Energized. More beautiful than she ever had before. More confident. She grazed a palm over her cheeks. They were completely smooth beneath the splatters of blood.

Paul checked for Sammy's pulse—absent. He approached Hannah like a predator to its prey. There was a hunger in his eyes as he closed the gap between them.

As he gazed at her, his eyebrows knit together. "You've never looked more beautiful."

She flashed a devilish grin as he whisked her into his arms, slamming her into the plastic-covered wall. As their lips met, her legs gripped tighter around his waist. He kissed her hard and repeatedly, each time more passionately than before. Their tongues tangled violently as their bodies melded together. She had become irresistible to Paul. Even after tearing every piece of clothing from her body and pressing himself deep inside her, he couldn't get enough. Their chests pressed together, enabling their racing hearts to align. His hand slipped and slid against the bloodied plastic as he fought to stay inside her with every thrust.

It didn't hurt like she'd thought it would. It was exhilarating. That night she had become his heroine, his girlfriend, and his everything. He had become her first.

SEVENTEEN

ADDISON

DECEMBER 2, 2024

It didn't feel safe to go home yet, Addison thought as she sat in her idling car. She had parked on the curb right outside Mrs. Wells's house. She knew her neighbor was home, as a royal-blue Cadillac CTS guarded the driveway. Chris had longstanding plans to visit his brother, which he'd insisted on canceling, but Addison knew they didn't get to see each other very often and had promised she would be okay. Veronica had offered for her to spend the night at her place, and Addison would call Chris immediately if anything happened, but first she needed to grab a few more things from home. Once she mustered up enough courage to go inside.

Last night's rainfall had become this morning's snow, blanketing the yards in a thin layer of white powder. Sunlight pierced through sparse trees, glistening against the freshly plowed asphalt and threatening to wipe away any evidence that it had snowed.

Across the street, the crimson house stared back at

Addison. It looked the same as it always had, yet vastly different. Ghosts of tragic memories peered from the windows, happy ones linked beside them. It was home. A home that now felt defiled. Every time she looked at it, it seemed like a creepy house. In her gut she knew someone was in there. Probably not anymore, she hoped. However, despite a brief meditation session, she wasn't quite ready to find out yet.

Ping. She retrieved her phone, heart racing. Could it be Unknown watching her again? She pictured him gazing down on her from behind the curtain in her parents' bedroom. If she squinted hard enough, she could almost see a shadowy figure. She shook the thought away, taking a deep inhale and long exhale, and forced herself to think positive thoughts. That's what Veronica would tell her to do. Maybe it was Tye, finally responding to her message. When she hadn't heard from him after their last date, she'd sent him a message asking him out for dinner.

Knowing the what-ifs could multiply indefinitely if she didn't set them to rest, she unlocked her screen.

MRS. WELLS

Hi honey, I think that's you parked outside. Is everything ok? Would you like to come inside?

ADDISON

I'll be right there.

The engine quieted and she climbed out, strategically arranging the longest key between her two middle fingers as a weapon. Just in case. Snow crunched and squeaked beneath her boots as she followed the now-hidden walkway by memory and mounted the steps to Mrs. Wells's house.

Before she could knock, the door swung open, releasing a swell of warmth and essential oils. Lavender and eucalyptus. Mrs. Wells's silver bangles pressed against Addison's back as she guided her into the foyer.

"Come, come, I just made some tea." Mrs. Wells slipped through a corridor on the left into the sitting room. Her deep-purple kimono robe caught the wind, fluttering with grace as she glided like a ghost.

The sitting room was Addison's favorite of all the rooms she had been in. It was the one room that hadn't changed at all since she was a kid and the room that Mrs. Wells always brought her in to make her feel better. Like Mrs. Wells's robe, the room was decorated in various shades of purple.

Romantic floral wallpaper with dark-purple petals and emerald-green leaves lifted the eye toward lilac crown molding with an intricate laurel pattern. There were two couches opposite each other, both upholstered in royal-purple tufted velvet. Between the couches, the focal point of the room, was a large polished amethyst geode serving as a coffee table. From what Addison remembered, Mrs. Wells had picked it up in Zambia during her travels. As in the other rooms, the walls were speckled with paintings. Artists like Marc Chagall and Pablo Picasso graced the walls with the childlike charm of their expressionism. Addison admired their ability to make dread so bold and colorful.

On the glass top of the amethyst coffee table sat a Victorian-style sterling silver teapot steaming with lavender tea. Addison always knew the type of tea being served based on the tablescaping Mrs. Wells did. Fresh and dried lavender had been placed with care around matching teacups and saucers. Lace and crystals were staged alongside.

With her belly and soul warmed by the tea, Addison's anxiety began to melt away before she even began discussing the recent events.

"Who do you think could have been in your house?" Mrs. Wells asked, her eyes blazing with concern.

"I think it must have been whoever this Unknown person is," Addison admitted as she continued to spill everything to Mrs. Wells. She and Chris had promised to keep everything between themselves, and she intended to, but this was different. Mrs. Wells had stepped up where she could when Addison's mother left.

And right now, Addison ached with the desperation of needing her mom. With the longing for all of her problems to be swept away by the comfort of a mother's touch. Addison needed her mom but would have to settle for the next-best thing.

"Have you heard from this Unknown person since the car crash?" Mrs. Wells refilled their teacups.

Addison thought for a moment. "Well, no, actually." A beat, then she continued. "But if that was Unknown in the crash . . . if Unknown was Jack, they would be dead."

"So it would have to be someone else?"

"I guess so."

"Do you know for sure that the accident that killed Jack was the same accident you witnessed?"

Addison pulled out her phone and Googled *Jack Waterford dead*. Immediately, several local news articles populated the screen. The first one, from the *Redlands Post*, read "Man Dead in Fiery Crash." Below, *Jack Waterford* was highlighted, indicating that his name was included in the article. When Addison opened it, a picture of the mangled black sedan next to a semi truck caused a brief flashback that sent a chill down her spine. It was Jack Waterford who had died chasing her. He was survived by his wife Jane and their daughter Celine.

"Are you okay, honey?" Mrs. Wells reached for Addison's hand across the table.

Addison didn't know what she was feeling. It was a jumbled mix of emotions. A little bit of relief, a little bit of sadness, and a lot more questions. Addison wanted to shout. Could his wife Jane be *the* Jane Thatcher? She refrained from blurting out the question. It was imperative that she find a balance between sharing just enough to receive advice while still protecting Mrs. Wells from Darkside.

"Yes, I'll be okay," Addison assured her neighbor, squeezing Mrs. Wells's hand back and finishing the last sip of her tea. "Thank you for always being there for me."

"Oh, it's my pleasure, sweetheart." Mrs. Wells radiated with elation, her hand navigating toward her warm heart. "You truly are like the daughter I never had but always wanted. I want you to know you are always welcome here. If you're too scared to go home, you can stay the night here anytime."

Addison choked on her words. "Thank you. I really appreciate that." She smiled, forcing the tears back into their respective ducts. "I'm going to stay with Veronica tonight—I already made plans with her—but I might take you up on your offer later this week."

After a quick cleanup and a bout of small talk, Mrs. Wells saw Addison out with a wave. Veronica's house was less than a five-minute drive away, which eliminated the need for a text or phone call.

———

Unlike Addison, Veronica didn't live in her childhood home, but she did live on the same street as her parents. There had been a time Addison was jealous of how close Veronica was to her parents, but over the years the jealousy had turned into admiration. Mr. and Mrs. Gonzales had provided her with the best example of what good parents looked like: loving, interested, and present. The kind of parent Addison vowed she would be if she ever decided to have kids. They helped fill the gaps that Mrs. Wells couldn't by rebuilding the broken pieces of her heart—like in kintsugi, the Japanese art of mending areas of breakage with gold. Another way she worked to find the gold lining amid life's tragedies. Silver had never been her color.

In a sea of Craftsman-style homes painted in neutrals, one house stood out. It was black, with carved spiderweb detailing in the corners of the porch where the columns met the roof. Tinted windows gave the house an even more sinister appearance, a beautiful contrast against the fresh snow. A black-cat wind chime sang with a burst of wind, just loud enough for Addison to hear it through her open windows as she drove up the street.

Veronica's house had come into view but was still a few houses down when Addison noticed something peculiar. Something that compelled her to pull over immediately and park, leaving her enough distance to see and just enough not to be seen.

Tye's car was parked in the driveway. If he drove a common car like a Corolla, she wouldn't speculate that it was him, but he didn't: He drove a burnt-orange Chevy Nova. The only thing more obvious would be a neon marque exclaiming *TYE IS HERE.*

Thoughts raced in her mind as she fought to push away the negative possibilities and reach for the positive. But it was quite a reach to come up with a positive reason that made any sense. Addison gripped the edge of her seat as the front door swung open, and she didn't have to use her imagination any longer.

Tye and Veronica emerged from the house, holding hands and smiling. Veronica wore a baggy shirt, boxers, and cheetah-print slippers, and Tye wore what had likely been last night's outfit. She tugged at his hand before he descended the steps. He swirled back around, scooping her up into his arms and leaning in for a kiss. Just like on a Hallmark film, they were giddy with love nouveau. Then came the walk of shame to his car, but there was no shame on his face—on either of their faces. It was more like a walk of satisfaction.

Rage pulsed inside Addison, causing her to tremble as she reached for the gearshift and rammed her car into drive. She was too mad to even cry. Usually, her instinct was to call Veronica when she was upset, but she couldn't even do that. Deep inhale, long exhale. Even more upsetting, she couldn't smoke a blunt to calm her rage. Her marijuana was still at her house, one of the reasons she'd wanted to go back.

She needed to vent to someone, but she couldn't call Chris. She wasn't ready to tell him about Tye, even though it was so over.

"Hey," Norah said breathily.

"Did I wake you up?" Addison had forgotten Norah was on shift that night.

"No, it's okay. I have been hitting snooze for a while." Norah's sheets rustled, indicating she was getting up.

"Veronica and Tye are hooking up," Addison said bluntly.

"What?" Norah exclaimed. If she wasn't awake before, she certainly was now.

"I drove over to her house to spend the night and saw him leaving her place."

"Maybe he was just helping her with something," Norah rationalized.

"She jumped in his arms and they kissed."

"What the hell," Norah fumed.

"I knew something was going on when he hadn't

texted me back after our last date, but I never thought he was sleeping with my best friend."

"I'm so sorry, and so in shock," Norah said as her coffeemaker gurgled and growled. "This isn't like her."

"That's why it's even more insane," Addison said. "I would have never expected her to do something like this, especially to me."

"Are you going to confront her?"

"Eventually," Addison replied. "If I ever talk to her again."

"Well, at least wait until you're a little more calm if you do," Norah urged. "Where are you going to stay tonight?"

"Mrs. Wells offered," Addison said. "It makes the most sense to stay there."

"Oh, that's perfect. I was going to say you can crash at my place, but you'll probably be more comfortable there." Norah lived in a studio apartment that felt more like a storage unit.

"By the way," Addison began, "thank you for forcing me to put those cat knuckles on my key ring. They may have saved my life."

"What do you mean?" Norah squealed with confusion and excitement.

"It's kind of a long story, and I'm sure you're already going to be late for work, but I promise to bring you up to speed as soon as possible."

"At least tell me what you used them on." Norah paused. "Or who."

"I used them to pop someone's tires," Addison said.

"Nice," Norah replied. "Well, please be careful, Addison, and please update me when you have a chance."

After they hung up, Addison texted Chris to notify him of the change in plans.

———

Later that evening, Addison returned to Mrs. Wells's house, where she found herself back in the sitting room for another therapeutic tea session. Chamomile this time. Two sessions in one day—any more and she would need to start looking for a therapist.

"I can't believe Veronica would do that," Mrs. Wells said. Shock washed over her face as if she were a baker who's cake had just been smashed.

"I can't either. Of all people, I would have never thought she would do something like this to me." Addison bit down on her anger.

"There has to be a good explanation," Mrs. Wells started. "Sorry, *good* isn't the best word, but there must be a reason."

"Maybe there is a reason," Addison said, "but I will never know what it is."

"So you're just never going to talk to her again?" Mrs. Wells's look of disappointment stung. Whose side was she on?

"No, I don't plan to." Addison downed the rest of her tea.

"Don't you think that's a little harsh?"

"No, I think what *she* did was harsh."

"Can I tell you something that you may not like to hear but that I think you need to hear?" Mrs. Wells asked.

"Yeah." Addison couldn't say no.

"You've been on, what, two dates with this guy? But you've been friends with Veronica since you were a kid. Two dates isn't long enough to have anything serious with someone. And, by the way you've talked about things, I don't think you even like him as much as you like the idea of him. Not to mention I don't think you would have continued to see Chris if you felt serious about Tye."

"It isn't even about Tye, honestly; it's the fact that Veronica didn't check with me first."

Mrs. Wells offered a comforting side hug. "Oh, honey, I know. And I'm not trying to diminish your feelings; I would feel the same way if I were in your shoes. You owe it to her, though, to at least explain herself before you write her off completely. She's more than just a friend to you; she's like a sister."

Addison knew Mrs. Wells was right, but her choice of words was like salt in an already stinging wound.

"I just need time to think." Addison pulled at a loose string on her jeans.

"That's understandable. Maybe tomorrow you'll be ready after you've rested. Come on, I'll show you to the guest room."

Mrs. Wells led Addison upstairs, every third step creaking along the way. Despite knowing Mrs. Wells for almost thirty years, Addison had never seen the second floor before. It had always been the forbidden zone. As a child, her imagination had been much more vibrant. Initially, she'd believed there was a mythical creature hiding up here, one that Mrs. Wells had brought home from Indonesia or Africa. Then the creature had devolved into hidden treasure. Now Addison had settled on the assumption that there were valuables Mrs. Wells didn't want a clumsy kid to destroy. Still, a streak of rebellion bolted through her as she mounted the final step and surfaced into a whimsical hallway that was just as bold as the rest of the house.

The walls in the hallway were covered in statement wallpaper sandwiched between crisp white molding. Upon a white backdrop, snakes, snails, and mice crawled along twigs and branches. Flowers and leaves added soft pops of color. Two rooms were on the right side of the hall and one primary suite was on the left, all with matching crystal doorknobs. The first door on the right offered Addison a peek at a lemon- and lime-themed bathroom.

A dragonfly Tiffany lamp illuminated the guest room. Mrs. Wells turned down the bed, stacking light-blue decorative pillows in the corner of the room. Addison quickly ran over to help. The room had a French feel to it, doused in soft blue and white with lace accents.

"This is so cool," Addison whispered.

"What's that?" Mrs. Wells asked as she fluffed a striped pillow.

"I always wondered what it looked like up here, and now I'm finally getting to see." Addison found herself in front of the mirrored closet. On the floor, tucked between the closet and a claw-foot dresser, was a large framed wedding photo.

"Who is this?" Addison asked as she impulsively pulled the picture out to get a better look.

"That's me," Mrs. Wells replied, joining Addison by the closet to reminisce.

"I didn't know you were married." Addison analyzed the photo. Mrs. Wells was young and beautiful. Her hair was long, blonde, and wavy, with natural body, and her skin was olive. A sleek wedding dress with wide bell sleeves highlighted her form, both simple and timeless. Despite the elegance of the dress, Mrs. Wells maintained her Bohemian image. Her husband wore a brown tuxedo, thick sideburns, and a mustache.

"That was a long time ago," Mrs. Wells said, running her finger down the length of her wedding gown.

"What happened to him, if you don't mind me asking?"

"Not at all," she said. "He passed away from lung cancer before you were born."

"I'm sorry," Addison said.

"Oh, it's okay, honey. That was a different time." Mrs. Wells smiled. "It was a very short marriage."

"It's so weird to see this; I've always just known you as Mrs. Wells, but I never really thought about there being a Mr. Wells." Addison returned the photo to its spot.

"I wasn't always Mrs. Wells." She made her way to the doorway.

"What was your maiden name?" Addison sat at the edge of the bed.

"Thatcher," Mrs. Wells said.

"Lucille Thatcher?" Addison replied, though it sounded more like a question.

"Jane Thatcher," she said as she pulled the door closed. "Lucille is my middle name."

Addison felt the color drain from her face, and her body went cold.

EIGHTEEN
ADDISON

ADDISON'S STOMACH twisted into knots as she watched the door. Instinct nudged her to lock it or, even better, run. Then she remembered that Mrs. Wells—Jane— didn't know everything, only the things Addison had shared with her. *She doesn't know that I know.* She remembered the line from her favorite *Friends* episode. There had been no discussion of Darkside of the Rainbow— certainly no discussion of Jane Thatcher or the fact that she was the cofounder of the cult.

Unless she did know. *Could Mrs. Wells be Unknown?* All of Addison's feelings of panic and anxiety flooded back in like high tide, and just as mussels cling to rock, her stomach tightened.

With all of her being, she wanted to call Veronica. She walked over to the window, where she peered out at her house. Suddenly, she felt she would be safer over there. The curtains sashayed back into place as Addison returned to the bed, her phone now lying beside her unlocked. Chris was at the top of her recent messages, then Veronica, then Unknown. Her thumbs tapped violently against the screen as she crafted a message for Chris, then deleted it. For just a moment, a wave of relief washed over her, knowing he had brought the satchel with him to his brother's house. To think she could have brought it into the lion's den. She shuddered. Chris was finally visiting his family, and she didn't want to disturb him. They were probably several beers deep into a game of Monopoly or chess by now. However, he had said he wanted to know if she found anything else out.

Swift thumbs reconstructed the text.

ADDISON

Chris, I'm really sorry to bug you while you're visiting, but I just found out something huge and I don't even know how to process it . . . Mrs. Wells is Jane Thatcher.

She waited for a reply, but only for a minute.

CHRIS

Your neighbor?!?

ADDISON

Yes! I've literally known her my entire life but had no clue she was in a freaking cult.

CHRIS

You didn't know her real name? Also, maybe she isn't involved with DOTR anymore. All of those murders were from back in the 70s.

ADDISON

No, I always thought her name was Lucille Wells, but apparently that was her middle/married name.

CHRIS

Yeah, that's possible. As far as we know the murders ended in the 70s . . .

Where are you now?

ADDISON

I'm in the guest room in her house.

CHRIS

WTF! Does she know you know?

I thought you were supposed to stay at Veronica's

ADDISON

Idk, I don't think so. Unless she is also Unknown.

Something came up with Veronica and Mrs. Wells offered me her guest room

CHRIS

Have you tried texting unknown again? We still don't know if it was Jack or not right?

ADDISON

I haven't, but I can. One sec . . .

Quickly, she swiped back to her messages, finding the conversation between her and Unknown.

ADDISON

Are you still there?

UNKNOWN

. . .

Back to Chris.

ADDISON

They're typing something . . . so I guess it wasn't Jack.

Back to Unknown.

UNKNOWN

Miss me already?

ADDISON

I was hoping you were dead.

Addison shivered after she hit send. Her message sounded much darker than she intended, but it was true nonetheless.

UNKNOWN

I am very much alive, something you may not be able to say if you don't cooperate.

ADDISON

Who are you?

UNKNOWN

In due time.

Back to Chris.

ADDISON

They're threatening to kill me if I don't cooperate.

CHRIS

I won't let that happen. Do you think it's Mrs Wells? Or Jane . . .

ADDISON

I don't know, but I'm scared to leave the room now. Especially if it is her threatening to kill me.

CHRIS

You need to get out of there just in case. I'm coming to get you.

ADDISON

No, I don't want you leaving early for me. You guys have been planning for this trip for over a year, you need to visit. I want you to visit. I can handle myself.

CHRIS

Don't worry about that, they will understand. Your safety is my priority. I can get there in a couple of hours, keep the door locked.

Addison's lips parted. He wanted to rescue her, and she wanted to let him.

ADDISON

Aw, thank you Chris. But really, I'll be ok. If I feel like I'm in danger, I'll leave. I promise.

Plus, Mrs. Wells is older now, I'm pretty sure I could take her if it came to that.

CHRIS

Ok, but promise you'll call me if anything
happens!

I'm sure you can stay at Veronica's even
if she's not there.

ADDISON

Yeah, true. If anything seems remotely
dangerous, I will get out of here right
away, I promise.

Veronica was the last person Addison wanted to see, but in all honesty, she knew she was capable of putting everything aside for one night if her life depended on it. Their friendship had overcome hurdles in the past. Those hurdles, however, didn't trip her up like this one.

Addison's eyes darted back to the door. She couldn't help but imagine the handle turning. Mrs. Wells would lunge toward her, arms outstretched and ready to latch on to Addison's throat. If only she knew where Mrs. Wells was. *A real-life version of the marauder's map from* Harry Potter *would be perfect,* she thought, realizing she watched way too much television. Acting normal was vital. It was imperative that she make it seem like nothing had changed between them, even though, in reality, *everything* had changed. It was too soon to determine the breadth of what that meant, but it caused her stomach to churn nonetheless.

She gently peeled her body from the bed, taking care to not rattle any springs or blankets. Delicate tiptoes guided her toward the door, which she locked as quietly as possible.

In an instant the room felt small, like a cage or a jail cell. If it became necessary, she could climb out the window and leave, but that would be too obvious—an option reserved for a true emergency. Instead, she chose to stay. Bide her time. Explore the room. Think of a legitimate excuse to leave without sleeping over. Maybe even return to her house.

Old clothes filled the dresser drawers, which smelled of mothballs. No hidden money or diaries. Neither nightstand had drawers; they were just elegantly carved walnut tables tasked with holding two matching touch lamps. There was nothing hidden under the bed, not even storage bins or wrapping paper. Faced with an unsettling feeling of déjà vu, Addison turned toward the closet, blowing a loose strand of hair from her face.

Addison slid open the left side of the closet to expose a bin of wrapping paper and stationery and several hanging winter coats. Quickly thumbing through the stationery, she found blank cards for every occasion, blank note paper, and gift tags. Nothing of interest.

On the other side of the closet was a tall black safe with a key pad and a five-point handle that spun to open. Keeping her promise, Addison snapped a picture and texted it to Chris.

CHRIS

Whoa, I wonder what she's hiding in there.

ADDISON

Me too, but I'm kinda scared to find out. What do you think the code could be?

CHRIS

Probably some sort of date. Do you
know her birthday or the date of her
wedding?

ADDISON

No, she didn't say what the date of her
wedding was, I do know her birthday
though… one sec

Addison punched in the numbers 3-17-54. Red light.
03-17-1954. Red light. 3-17-1954. Nothing but a red
light and a fruitless tug.

ADDISON

Nope, no luck.

CHRIS

What about the date of that Pink Floyd
concert

ADDISON

Oooh, that's a good idea

She tried every variation of 06-17-1973 without
success. She tried her birthday. Veronica's birthday. Even
Norah's. Defeat gripped her, as she was unable to think
of any other important dates.

ADDISON

Nothing is working

CHRIS

What was that other picture you sent
me? The clue you went back to Rusty
Tavern for . . .

ADDISON

OMG, you think that could be it?

CHRIS

Anything is possible

ADDISON

That seems too easy

CHRIS

Unless Unknown wants you to find
whatever is inside

Addison pulled up the picture she had taken of the fortune cookie paper with the numbers *1, 0, 1, 9, 7, 6.* She punched them in. Green light. With a quick spin and a pull, the door to the safe was open. Her pulse quickened.

ADDISON

I'm in!

CHRIS

What do you see?

Reaching in, Addison pulled out a pristine copy of *The Official Handbook of the Darkside of the Rainbow.* She repositioned herself on the floor into a spot more conducive to reading. Flipping through the pages, she snapped a few random pictures and texted them to Chris.

CHRIS

Well, that definitely confirms it, not that
we needed any other proof

The book was far too thick to read in its entirety, but

she attempted to find any pages that particularly stood out. Page 52, titled "Rituals," revealed detailed instructions on how to receive divine messages through music. Backmasking was the best way and the most reliable, according to the text.

While scanning through, Addison learned that listening to music in reverse during the "witching hour"—which a quick Google search revealed was between three and four a.m.—was optimal for receiving. While all forms of media were appropriate, listening to vinyl was the advisable way to receive messages. Candles *must* be lit, preferably right when the clock struck the hour. While the witching hour itself was a time when the veil between the spiritual realm and the human world was thin, ingesting psychotropic drugs during the ritual would enhance the listener's ability to connect and receive.

The book went into much more detail, including the best types of psychotropic drugs, specific chants, and how to use a Ouija board during rituals for precision.

Flipping forward, Addison landed on a section detailing the differences between intentional messages and unintentional messages. Oftentimes, unintentional messages were placed into the music by spirits without the knowledge of the artists. Intentional messages, on the other hand, were most commonly placed by artists who actively devoted themselves as a vessel to receiving and transmitting the messages of the divine. *Their version of the divine,* Addison thought, knowing what they worshipped was something evil. She wasn't perfect, but she believed in her heart that there was a God. A divine creator. The God she believed in would never influence people to hide messages in music that led to murder and destruction.

Slippered feet shuffled outside the door. Addison shut the book and sat as still as possible, not daring to even swallow. Moments later a door shut. Then came the muffled sound of a shower squeaking on. Tension released from her muscles, allowing her to swallow the saliva that had built up in her mouth. She tucked the book back into the safe, fighting the urge to take it with her. If she did take it and Mrs. Wells went looking for it, she would know with certainty who took it.

At the top of the safe was a small cubby with a little black box tucked in the back. Addison shimmied the lid opened. The contents caused her to gasp, almost fumbling the box, but she caught it. What was Mrs. Wells doing with a black, necrotic index finger? A wave of nausea trickled through her body, both from the smell and from a realization she hoped wasn't true.

Her mind flashed back to the last moments she'd spent with her patient. The last flicker of life that widened his eyes. The war cry of the ICU alarms, warning of impending doom. His firm and final grip on her forearm. What was left of his fingers digging into her sensitive skin. He had been missing the index finger on his left hand down to the middle knuckle. Was Addison 100 percent sure that this was his finger? No. That would require forensics. But it was pretty damning evidence.

Her phone silently snapped a photo, and naturally, she sent it to Chris.

CHRIS

WTF! Is that what I think it is?

ADDISON

Yes, it is most definitely a finger. I think it might be my patient's finger. He was missing part of his index finger, but I just assumed he was a carpenter or something.

CHRIS

I don't think you should stay there. Jane is clearly dangerous.

ADDISON

Ugh, you're right, but I can't just walk out, she is going to question why I left and probably will know I found the safe

CHRIS

She probably is the one that wanted you to find the safe. We know someone did or else they wouldn't have led you to the combination.

Make sure you put everything back exactly how you found it. If you can't think of an excuse just climb out the window. Please be careful, babe! And if anything goes wrong, I will come get you immediately. Our safe word will be .

. .

Rainbow emoji. Send me like five rainbow emojis right now so it will come up in your recently used emojis, in case you need to send it quickly.

Addison complied with his request, her cheeks flushed. That was the first time he had called her babe.

After tucking the box back in the cubby exactly how she'd found it, she looked back at the bottom of the safe, checking for anything she might have missed. The glint of a small silver revolver with pearl grips caught her eye. Touching it was out of the question. The last thing she needed was one of her fingerprints showing up on a murder weapon. Could that be the gun her patient was shot with?

She silently snapped another photo. Before putting everything back in place, she retrieved a folded-up letter from the back corner.

Jane,

I have taken care of him, I hope this finger is proof enough. I am not happy with your request, in fact, I found your letter to be quite disrespectful after all we have been through. Haven't I proven myself enough with all I've done for the group? How much or how little I drink is none of your concern. My life outside of the group is none of your business, that includes my daughter. I see you watching her. Waiting to get your hands on her. She is never going to live the same life we all have. She is going to become someone important and leave all of this behind. You'll see. But now, because of you, she will have to go on living the rest of her life without a father. And what's worse, she will think he chose to leave her. For that, I will never forgive you. I will do everything I can to protect her from you and I will spend my life protecting her from our secrets. Next time you see me having more drinks than I probably should, do us both a favor and mind your own business. Thank you for your understanding. I will see you at the round table.

Devotedly,
Hannah Garver

NINETEEN
ADDISON

Addison's throat tightened. Was her patient her dad? Was that how he'd known her name before ever meeting her? How he'd left the recording on the cassette specifically for her? How could Mrs. Wells have looked her in the eyes all those years and never shared any of this information? The questions kept tumbling to the front of her mind, one after the other, like dominoes. Questions that Mrs. Wells likely held all the answers to. Addison felt sick. She wanted to scream. It was as though her entire world had been tipped off its axis, spiraling out of control. It was hard enough that she couldn't save her patient's life, but now it was her dad's life she couldn't save. Her loyalty to him, to his mission, grew stronger.

She pushed the turbulent thoughts to the back of her mind, then gently slid the closet door shut. It was time to close up the bed, situate the decorative pillows back in place, and smooth out the linens. Time to make an exit.

Deep inhale, long exhale. With a soft twist of the

crystal doorknob, she emerged into the hall. Part of her expected Mrs. Wells to be right there waiting for her, knife raised high overhead against the backdrop of screeching violins, but she wasn't. Addison peered down the hall. *She must be asleep,* Addison thought, taking note of the closed primary bedroom door as she proceeded to the steps on her tiptoes.

A loud creak jolted her, disarming her stealth. Under her breath, she cursed the stairs. A siren might as well have gone off.

"Addison?" a voice called out from below.

"Yes," Addison replied as she scurried down the final steps into the foyer. There was no longer a need to be quiet.

"Is everything okay?" Mrs. Wells asked, approaching Addison from the dining room.

"Veronica called," Addison lied. "After thinking about everything you said, I decided to answer and give her a chance to explain. She asked me to come over so we can talk about everything in person."

"I'm glad you two are talking again," Mrs. Wells said. Addison swore Mrs. Wells's gaze penetrated deeper than usual, like she was studying her. Assessing her expressions and tone to determine what she knew.

"Thank you so much for offering the guest room to me, but I think I'm going to go over to Veronica's and try to work this out." She shuffled toward the front door. Her heart picked up its pace. All that stood between betrayal and freedom was the clunky wooden door.

"Of course, honey." Mrs. Wells drifted closer,

extending a hand now absent of jewelry, squeezing Addison's shoulder almost too tightly. "I think that's a wonderful idea. The guest room is always open to you if you ever need it."

Addison tugged at the door. It wouldn't budge. She tugged harder, twisted the lock on the knob, and jiggled the handle. Heat plumed inside her chest along with a sinking feeling, like a geyser erupting and falling.

Mrs. Wells sensed Addison's panic like a dog. If Addison had been paying more attention, she would have caught the sly smirk that carved itself into Mrs. Wells's face. The sour side of her that she kept bottled up so nicely.

"Honey, the dead bolt," Mrs. Wells offered.

Addison paused to recalibrate, then reached for the dead bolt, giving it a twist. Success. She tugged the door open and felt the cold of night smack her in the face, activating her sympathetic nervous system.

Gentle steps evolved into a sprint. She could still feel Mrs. Wells's eyes on her. Her car roared to a start, smoke bellowing from behind and swirling in the glow of the red taillights. Windshield wipers swished the fresh snow away, enabling Addison to have a clear view of Mrs. Wells's house and her own. They faced each other like opponents, competing for creepiest house. Her traveling eyes caught a glimpse of a figure standing at the window of the guest room. The room she was just in. Straining to see, Addison leaned forward into the steering wheel. It wasn't the silhouette of an older woman. It was the silhouette of a man. A tall man. There had been someone else in the house the entire time, and she'd had no idea. What if he was Unknown? What if he was the one who had been in her house?

Chills crawled down her spine as she sped away. The five-minute drive turned into a two-minute drive. Her tires rolled to a stop in the driveway next to Veronica's black BMW. Bat decals swept across the back window. Very Veronica.

Satie's Gnossienne No. 3 danced through the house at the tap of the doorbell, ringing out longer than any doorbell should. Bright but ominous, the minor-key composition was beautiful on the surface yet concealed a mystery beneath. Addison felt this mirrored her friend well.

Veronica yawned as she slowly opened the door. Her black hair was secured in rollers, her eyes tired and her body draped in a black satin nightgown and matching robe that she pulled tighter. Her feet were snug inside leopard-print slippers.

"Addy?" Veronica said, the excitement in her voice succumbing to fatigue. It was only eleven p.m.

"Hey, Ronnie, can I stay here tonight?" Addison felt like a stray dog.

"Come in, what's going on? Why didn't you call?" She rubbed her eyes as she led Addison into the kitchen.

LED lights glowed pink beneath the cabinets, bright enough to illuminate the room without being too harsh. Veronica's kitchen was the perfect mix of modern and retro. Pink appliances designed to look like they were made in the 1950s accompanied white cabinets with silver pulls. White quartz countertops glistened. Veronica had added touches of her personality as if by the wave of a magic wand: a Bettie Page paper towel holder; a spiderweb soap dispenser that she and Addison had bought together at Home Goods during Halloween one year. Addison and Norah had matching dispensers under their kitchen sinks. A zombie pinup girl dish towel hung from the stove, and a handful of rockabilly-themed magnets spread across the fridge.

"Chris is staying over at his brother's house," Addison said as she received a glass of water from Veronica and sat on a barstool at the island.

"I know, I thought you were going to come over earlier."

"I was, but I decided to stop by Mrs. Wells' house first and ended up staying late." Addison sipped her water.

Veronica stood at the sink opposite Addison. "Well, I'm glad you're here, for a few reasons. First, of course, because I missed you and love seeing you. But"—she hesitated—"there's actually something I need to tell you that I'm scared to tell you."

Addison's heart quickened. "What is it?" She was sure she already knew what was coming.

Veronica sucked in a deep breath of air. "I don't know how to say this."

"Veronica, just say it," Addison pressed with a touch of attitude that snapped like a rubber band.

"Okay, well, I kind of hooked up with Tye." She ran over to Addison's side, preparing to beg for forgiveness.

There was no shock value. Addison replied flatly, "I know."

"You do?" Veronica stood up straight. The color drained from her face.

"Yes." Addison swiveled to face Veronica. "I drove over here this morning, and when I was pulling up, I saw him leaving your house."

Veronica's eyes widened. "I'm so sorry, Addison." Her plea was visible in her eyes, her quivering bottom lip, and her trembling hands.

"Why would you do that to me? How could you?" Addison shook her head.

"I know, I know." Veronica's hands thrust to her face, pulling her eyelids down with angst. "I don't even know what I was thinking. I wasn't thinking. We had this weird connection the night we met at the bar . . ."

"During *my* date with him?" Addison interjected.

"Yes, during your date." Veronica's face scrunched up. "God, I'm a terrible person, I know."

"I knew he was ghosting me, but I didn't think it was because he was sleeping with my best friend." Addison looked away.

"I didn't know how to tell you. I was hoping you'd just continue to focus on Chris and forget about Tye," Veronica said.

"I mean, I kind of have, but that's not the point," Addison said. "It's the principle. You were supposed to be my best friend, the one person I could trust in this world, and you betrayed me."

Judging by Veronica's expression, her words stung like a wasp.

"Who made the first move?" Addison asked.

"He did." Her face wilted into a frown, pity saturating her stare.

"How did he even get your number?"

"We added each other on Instagram that night, and he contacted me the next day," Veronica said. A beat. "We got to talking; I was trying to be friendly, trying to make sure he was a good guy if he was going to become something serious in your life. One thing led to another—"

"It always does," Addison snarked.

"Anyways," she emphasized, "we had a lot in common. I've never connected with anyone like this before. I felt so torn—I didn't want to hurt you, but I also have been alone for so long now. It felt good to be seen and admired. It felt good to connect in a way I have never connected with anyone before."

"So you two are soulmates, then?" Addison glared.

"He might be one of my soulmates," Veronica admitted. "You know I believe that everyone has more than one soulmate out there, and if we're lucky, we'll find one."

"You barely met him! How could you be soulmates?" Addison spat.

"I just know."

"How?" Addison's face began to soften.

"When I'm with him, it feels natural, like he's a part of me existing outside of myself. We view life from the same lens, yet he brings back pieces of me that I didn't even know were missing. We can just sit on the couch and do nothing and I feel like everything is exactly how it should be." Veronica would have continued if Addison didn't stop her.

"I get it, but you have to know how crazy you sound." If Addison was being honest with herself, she did not feel those things for Tye. She found him extremely alluring and had a great time with him. He was a good kisser. Fun. Not a soulmate. She did, however, feel everything Veronica had described with Chris.

"A huge part of me is so sorry. I betrayed you, I hurt you, and I never thought I was capable of doing that to you." Veronica wrapped her arms around Addison, pressing deeper into Addison's resistance. "But there's this other part of me that isn't sorry, because I found someone that I've always dreamed of finding."

Addison twinged. It was a sharp apology.

"I do forgive you," Addison began, but quickly stopped Veronica's excitement with a raised finger, the same index finger her patient—her dad—was missing. She shook the image of his necrotic finger from her mind and continued *"But* I'm not happy about you not telling me right away. If you had just come to me from the beginning and explained your interest, I would have had the chance to say it was okay."

Veronica nodded in agreement. "I promise to always come to you in the future."

"You're lucky I'm not forcing you to sit inside a box to think about what you did, like Joey did to Chandler on *Friends,*" Addison poked.

"Oh God," Veronica laughed.

They hugged before heading upstairs to Veronica's room.

Veronica loved satin. Her curtains were satin. Her bedding was satin. If it wasn't satin, it was fur. Slipping and sliding into an upright position on the bed, the girls shimmied into a comfortable position, primed and ready for pillow talk.

"Did you go back home at all?" Veronica asked.

"No, I couldn't bring myself to go home yet," Addison replied, "I *was* going to come here, but you know . . ." Her voice trailed off.

"So what made you come here tonight then? Why didn't you just stay over at Mrs. Wells'?" Veronica looked confused.

Addison sighed. "Where do I even begin?" Not withholding any details, Addison filled her in.

Veronica gasped. "Your patient was your dad?"

"Yes, which is even more reason for me to figure out what the hell is going on," Addison remarked.

"So, wait." Veronica sat up and slid toward Addison, legs crisscrossed. "Does Mrs. Wells, or 'Jane'"—she used air quotes—"know that you know who she really is?"

"I don't think so." Addison pondered. "I did tell her a lot about what's going on, but I also left out a lot of details."

"I'm literally shook. I just cannot even imagine her being involved in something like this," Veronica said. "Did she act strange when you left?"

"I kind of felt like she did, but I also think I was just freaked out in general," Addison admitted.

"Do you think she still is involved in this cult stuff?"

"I'm not totally sure," Addison said, "but obviously someone is still involved in it, or else I wouldn't be getting these unknown texts and all these creepy clues. I'm just not sure if she's still an active member." A breath escaped her. "I just can't imagine the Mrs. Wells I know doing anything like that. How could she hide that side of her so well from someone so close to her?"

"Well, I guess people do things like that all the time, if we really think about it. Husbands keep affairs secret for months, even years," Veronica mused. "Maybe you should confront her."

Addison withdrew. "No way! If she's still an active member of Darkside, I'm not trying to get killed. It's better if she doesn't know that I know who she is. Right now I have the upper hand. Whatever that even means in this scenario." She thrust her head back, sinking deeper into the plush pillows and rubbing her face with a groan.

"Sometimes I just want to text Unknown and tell them they can have the key and just be done with all of this," Addison confessed.

"That is always an option, Addison." Veronica rested a supportive hand on her forearm. "I mean, if all of this continues to be dangerous, it might just be better to give them what they want. For your own safety."

Addison's heart and mind battled.

"For now, I'm going to keep pressing forward. I need

to figure out what my patient . . . what my dad was hiding," Addison decided.

"Well, I support whatever decision you make." Veronica reached over and turned out the light. "Just promise me you'll keep me updated on everything. I don't like when *Chris* knows more than me." Her voice flared when she said his name.

"Someone is jealous," Addison teased, triggering laughter. And just like that, they were back to normal.

Addison's phone buzzed. It was Chris.

CHRIS

Addy, check this out.

An attached link led her to a local news website. The headline read "Two Women Found Dead at Rusty Tavern Bar."

TWENTY
ADDISON

GRUESOME SCENE INDEED. Those were the exact words the woman on Channel 3 news used to describe the murder at the Rusty Tavern bar. It was gruesome—at least the parts Addison could see on Chris's flat-screen TV and in online news articles. The bodies had been found in different locations of the bar. One woman had been left atop a pool table, positioned with her arms and legs spread outward like the Vitruvian Man. A pool ball, which Addison later confirmed through research to be the eight ball, had been shoved into her mouth, dislocating her jaw. Blood pooled beneath her body, staining the cherry-colored felt a darker shade of red.

The other woman was dismembered. Her torso and head were found on the floor of the women's bathroom. Legs and arms were strewn about the bar, as though an animal had torn her apart limb by limb.

Addison had returned to Chris's apartment the following morning as soon as he got back into town, just as promised. Despite her objection, he came home a day earlier than he was supposed to. With his broken leg, he would have several weeks off of work and insisted that Addison stay with him until they figured out what her dad had been hiding. What Unknown wanted to find. They'd be safer together.

Curled up in the corner spot of the sectional, Addison flipped through all of the local news channels, hoping to find a new angle on the crime scene. A different interview. A clue. She knew time was limited. Evidence would be scrubbed, photos deleted, and testimonies buried.

"This has to be connected to Darkside, right?" Addison shouted, her thumb hovering over the channel button on the remote.

Chris was in the kitchen preparing dinner—smash burgers with his special sauce, which tasted exactly like Big Mac sauce. Addison suspected it was just Thousand Island dressing with a little extra ketchup. Whatever it was, she loved it and found herself craving it more and more.

Tossing the remote aside, she began scrolling on her phone. Meat sizzled behind her. Fresh onions and lettuce filled the air with a bright scent. Her mouth watered as she patiently and cozily waited for Chris to join her.

"Social media is showing a lot more than the news," Addison shouted over the sonorous growl of the vent fan.

"Like what?" Chris asked, handing Addison a burger on a paper plate and climbing under her blanket. He let his booted left leg hang out.

"Like this I found on Reddit." Addison zoomed in to an uncensored photo of the woman on the pool table. "Look at the marking on her forehead."

"Remember the letter your dad wrote about what had happened to your mom? He mentioned a marking exactly like this," Chris said, observing a blue triangle on the woman's forehead etched from cue chalk.

"I'm trying to see if there is anything else that could link these murders to Darkside of the Rainbow," Addison said, pausing for a moment to take a satisfying bite. With a new investigation open, perhaps whatever her patient had been hiding could help the police stop Darkside for good.

"What time are they saying these murders took place?" Chris asked.

She toggled to another tab and scrolled. "Twelve p.m."

"Was that before you went to Mrs. Wells' house?"

"Before I went back to her house," Addison said, then remembered he didn't know she had gone to Veronica's house.

"What do you mean, back?"

She hesitated. "I had parked outside, trying to decide if I wanted to go in my house to grab some things or if I should just go straight over to Veronica's, and I guess Mrs. Wells saw me. She texted me to come in. We had some tea and hung out for a little while, probably until about eleven, then I went to Veronica's."

Confusion gripped Chris's face, a slight rise of his left brow.

"I went to Veronica's, but before I could get out of my car, I . . ." She hesitated. "I saw Tye leaving her place, and they kissed."

"Who's Tye?" he interrupted.

"It's a guy I went on a couple dates with." Her pulse quickened.

"Recently?" Chris's body became tense.

"Yes, recently." She swallowed. "I introduced them, and apparently they exchanged information and hooked up behind my back."

He was silent. Processing.

"Chris"—she reached for his hand—"it was only a couple of dates; nothing ever got serious between us. But when I saw him leaving her place, I was pretty upset. I couldn't believe Ronnie would do something like that without asking if I was okay with it first."

"How recently?"

"Within the last few weeks." All of the guilt she had suppressed or avoided came rushing back.

"Please say something," Addison pleaded, grasping to hold his hand. He resisted.

"I-I don't even know what to say."

"Look at me," Addison said softly, and he did with a lamenting gaze.

"Did you sleep with him?"

"No," Addison said abruptly. The tension in his body began to release.

"I wasn't even mad that they hooked up; I was mad that she did it behind my back," she explained.

"I know we haven't really discussed our relationship, but I guess I just thought we were on the same page."

"We are." Her voice rose as she scooted closer, now cupping his hands in her own.

"I don't think we are, Addy. I thought we were exclusive. Anytime I talk about you, I refer to you as my girlfriend."

Her stomach sank. "I want to be your girlfriend; I just didn't think you wanted me to be. I didn't realize you felt that way."

Chris's mouth slackened, his eyes growing wide.

"How could you even think that?" he said.

"Well, for starters, you never asked me to be."

"We're almost thirty; I didn't think I needed to."

"We probably should have talked about this, huh?" Addison shot him a look of remorse. "I understand if you don't want me to be your girlfriend now."

"Stop." He pulled her closer. "I should have been more clear about how I feel about you. I'm not happy about you going out with another guy, but I'm not going to stop seeing you over it."

Addison smiled.

"Was there anyone else?"

"No, just Tye."

A heavy breath escaped him. "Let's clear up any confusion, then, and make this official. Addison, will you be my girlfriend?"

"Yes," she blurted, kissing him hard.

Chris smirked. "Good. Now that that's settled, let's get back to business. We need to focus."

"Okay, so after I saw Veronica and Tye, I called Norah, then went over to the Roast Office for a few hours. I listened to an audiobook and had a few cups of coffee. I didn't want to go right back to Mrs. Wells' house."

"What time did you end up going back?"

"Around six or six fifteen." Addison paused. "Do you think Mrs. Wells did this?"

"Well, not by herself; she would have needed help."

Addison gasped.

"What?" Chris shot up to come to her aid.

"When I left her place, I saw someone in the window upstairs. It looked like a man, but I couldn't quite make out the details. It for sure wasn't her, though, I know that."

"Was he in there the entire time you were there?" He clenched his jaw.

"I don't know. He could have been, or he could have gotten there right before I left. Either way, he must have been hiding the whole time." Addison shook off a chill.

"Why didn't you tell me?"

"Because if I told you, you would have left your brother's house right then, and I didn't want you to do that."

Addison's phone pinged.

UNKNOWN

Don't overlook this clue like you did the last. Some people without brains do an awful lot of talking . . . don't they?

> My head I'd be scratchin', my thoughts
> are busy hatchin', if only I had a brain.
>
> People with hearts have something to
> guide them, but I don't have a heart.

"I knew it was connected," Addison blurted, passing her phone to Chris.

"Whenever we find out who this is, I'm going to punch him. Or worse." Chris's nostrils flared.

"Hopefully, when we find out who this is, they will be thrown in prison," Addison remarked.

He handed the phone back to Addison. She returned to the Reddit tab she had been looking at prior to receiving the text message. "I came across something I think Unknown could be referring to. Check this out."

Reddit User Maine_man0233192

I am friends with one of the bartenders there and he mentioned some things in the Rusty Tavern murders that they aren't reporting on. The woman on the pool table was found with her brain missing. It was removed from the back of her head. The woman found in the bathroom was missing her heart, also removed through her back. The organs weren't found on the scene though. I think this is why they aren't reporting this anymore. I screenshot an article by a local newspaper that originally contained a statement by the police chief mentioning that organs were removed from the bodies. The article no longer exists.

"Unknown said people without brains do an awful lot of talking." Addison connected the dots. "She was found with a pool ball in her mouth."

"So she couldn't talk anymore," Chris finished.

"We need to find out who these women were," Addison said. "And what this woman knew that caused them to silence her."

TWENTY-ONE
ADDISON

DECEMBER 4, 2024

Sage-green sheets caressed Addison as if she were a stuffed grape leaf. Her naked body glided across the buttery Egyptian cotton sheets as she stretched the night from her. An indigo down comforter cascaded to the floor as she stood up, finding one of Chris's band tees to slip into on her way out of his room.

A fresh cup of black coffee awaited her in the kitchen. Chris flashed a white panoramic smile from beneath his now-trimmed beard. His tousled blond hair bounced, with one loose strand lingering in a malevolent but sexy manner over his right eye. The musculature of his arms and abdomen became more defined as he moved.

Tranquility flowed through Addison this morning. It was her first morning as Chris's girlfriend, a notion that made everything seem as though it would be all right. All of the adrenal fatigue and anxiety that had been tormenting her body was lifting like a kite, leaving her featherlight and carefree in the wind. And, for a moment, she forgot about everything.

Ping.

NOTIFICATION FROM CASABLANCA

She glanced at the lock screen of her phone before opening the app.

TYE

Hey Addison, I'm sorry I have been M.I.A. these past few days. Work has been crazy. Can we get together tonight? I really want to see you and have a lot to fill you in on.

The audacity, Addison thought.

"Why is he messaging you?" Chris asked from over her shoulder, startling her.

"I guess Veronica hasn't told him about our discussion yet."

Chris pulled away after lingering just long enough to read the message.

"Why don't you tell him?" Chris suggested, though it sounded more like a demand.

"I will." Addison began typing a reply. "I'll tell him things have gotten very serious with someone else, I'm in love, and I wish him the best."

Chris smiled, scooping her into his chest. "Very serious, huh?" he said. "And in love."

Addison rolled her eyes. "Don't push your luck."

"I'm in love too." He turned her around to kiss her.

During breakfast, Chris suggested they return to Addison's house and scope it out. It had been a couple of days since she'd been home. They could go together to see if anything was out of place or tampered with.

As they pulled into Addison's driveway, her eyes scanned the exterior of her house. Nothing appeared out of place. Sunlight warmed Addison's skin as she slammed the passenger door of Chris's car shut. He had already purchased a new car, since the accident had totaled his. A Dodge Challenger, black with dark-tinted windows. Cherry-red racing stripes traveled from the front of the car over the hood scoop, terminating at the trunk.

Glancing across the street, Addison noticed Mrs. Wells's Cadillac was gone. A sigh of relief escaped her. It made her feel slightly safer knowing *Jane Thatcher* wouldn't be watching them from her house.

The front door was locked, with no signs of forced entry or damage. Warmth gripped them as they stepped into the foyer, reminding Addison that she had left in such a hurry that the heater was still on. The air smelled of warmed carpet with a hint of clean linen, the fragrance of her favorite plug-in air freshener. It was one of those rare opportunities to experience the true scent of her home—like returning from a long vacation. Or, in Addison's case, returning from a breaking and entering.

Sticking together, they searched each room. They checked the windows for damage or disruption of any kind, but nothing was out of the ordinary. Downstairs in every window track, wooden sticks remained secure. No one was hiding in any of the closets or behind the curtains.

With every other part of the house cleared, it was time to check her parents' room, where she had first heard the culprit. A chill ran down Addison's spine as she observed the open door.

"This was closed last time I was here," she explained as they stepped inside. "I'm positive about that."

At first glance, the room looked undisturbed. Addison hadn't moved anything since the day her mom left. The bed was still made with Laura Ashley floral bedding. A Styrofoam cup stained with lipstick rested on the nightstand beside an overflowing ashtray. Dust permeated the air and seeped into the fabric. Addison noted that the room could use an air freshener.

"What could they have been doing in here?" Addison asked, approaching the dresser.

"It looks like someone may have rummaged through the closet," Chris said, prodding at a pile of fallen clothes on the floor.

Addison gasped. "I think I know what they took."

"What?" Chris approached her left.

The photo of her dad wasn't on the dresser anymore. In fact, it wasn't anywhere. It hadn't fallen beside or under the dresser. It wasn't moved to another spot. It was gone.

Addison's eyes met Chris's.

"Someone was in here, one hundred percent,"

Addison confirmed, "but why would they take that photo of my dad?"

"Maybe to hide any evidence that could point to Darkside existing?" Chris speculated. "Was there anything special about that specific photo?"

"It was just a picture of him standing in front of the factory he worked at," Addison said. "On the back of the photo, someone had written 'The great and terrible Oz,' which was also one of the things my patient . . . my dad . . . said to me before he coded."

"Was there anything else that stood out?"

"Just that he was wearing a 'Revolution 9' shirt," Addison said.

"Hmm." Chris thought for a moment. "Well, whoever took the photo must find it significant somehow." He gestured toward a small piece of paper wedged beneath a jewelry box. "What's that?"

Addison pulled it loose. In the same type of magazine cut-out letters as the previous note she had received, it read:

i couLd bE huMan . . . iF oNLY i
had a hEaRt.

Addison's breath accelerated. "I can't believe this is happening. They were in here while I was in here. I was literally in the next room over."

"Take a deep breath," Chris guided.

"I thought once I quit my job, my life would get easier. I would take time off and finally relax. But now this? When is it going to end?"

"We can call the police right now," Chris said. "We can tell them everything we know, and they can take over. They already have an open investigation on Darkside now with the Rusty Tavern murders. If we turn over everything we have, they can take care of the rest."

Addison sat on the edge of the bed and thought for a moment. It would be a relief. Taking her patient's things didn't seem so bad now that she'd found out he was her dad. The problem was that he *was* her dad. He'd entrusted her with his things. With his operation to stop them.

"No, it's okay. Let's keep going."

"Are you sure?" Chris asked.

"I'm sure."

They returned downstairs. Mounting the final steps, the front door came into view and Addison was bombarded with the memory of her escape.

"It's so violating," she confessed as they made their way to the kitchen. "Whoever was in here must have had a key, or else they are very good at picking locks."

A gentle back rub gave her solace.

"Want anything to drink before we head back?" Chris asked as he pried open the refrigerator door. Jarred by a waft of putrid air, he fell to the kitchen floor, losing balance on his broken leg. The door remained agape.

"What is that smell?" Addison inquired, holding her breath as she ran to help Chris up.

On the top shelf, side by side, rested a brain and a heart. Blood pooled beneath the lounging organs like a grisly oasis, spilling its contents to the shelves below.

"Are those . . . ?" Addison couldn't finish, as she was overcome by an overwhelming urge to throw up.

"They have to be." Chris scooted closer and slammed the door shut.

Addison bolted to the sink and retched.

TWENTY-TWO
ADDISON

Tightness enveloped Addison's throat as she began to dial 911.

"Wait." Chris grabbed Addison's hand. She could feel him quivering.

"What? You don't think we should call?" Addison closed the number pad.

"I think we should think about this more before we call," Chris explained, eyes darting around the room.

"What is there to think about? If we don't call, they're going to think we have something to do with this." Addison was right; they both knew this.

"Yes, but what if they're trying to frame you?" he asked. "Your dad told you these people are dangerous. They murdered people in the seventies and beyond without ever getting caught. Something like that doesn't happen without connections."

Addison was at a loss for words.

"Not to mention you will never be able to finish decoding his message if we call now."

"But if they aren't trying to frame me, and I don't call the police, I will for sure get in trouble. I can't just leave a brain and a heart in my fridge. Isn't that obstruction of justice or something?"

Chris ran his fingers through his hair and tugged.

Addison released a deep sigh and sat down at the kitchen table. "What other option do we have?"

"We can get rid of it," Chris offered.

"Get rid of it?" Addison jolted backward.

"Unknown is clearly trying to screw with you. Maybe we need to play along. Do something they wouldn't expect us to do."

"I can't believe you're saying this," Addison replied.

"I can't either."

Addison's face lit up as she darted toward the window, peeling the blinds open just enough for her to see. "Mrs. Wells is still gone."

"Okay," Chris said. "What does that have to do with anything?"

"What if we put them in her safe?" she suggested.

Chris paused for a moment. "That might actually work, but what if she comes back while you're in there? It's too dangerous."

"Well, you can't go with your leg like that," Addison pointed out. "You have to stay here and keep watch. I will plant them in the safe, and then I'll come back here and we can clean up the blood."

Together they worked out all the details and grabbed

supplies. Nitrile gloves from Addison's workbag. Plastic grocery bags Mrs. Wells had sent food over in, some still with the receipt. In the bottom of her workbag, Addison discovered a random pair of surgical shoe covers that she thought could work. Sifting through the kitchen junk drawer, she found the spare key Mrs. Wells had given her a few years back. Addison had been tasked with watering the plants while Mrs. Wells traveled the South of France.

Before removing the organs from the refrigerator, she and Chris laid down plastic trash bags. With triple-gloved hands and a PPE gown left over from COVID, Addison carefully slipped the heart and brain into a plastic grocery bag, then the whole thing inside another. She discarded the first layer of gloves, then with a firm tug, she tied the handles together.

Mrs. Wells's car was still gone. Addison dashed across the street and let herself in, locking the door behind her. She paused and listened. All she could hear was the ringing in her own ears. Deep inhale, long exhale.

Her gut twisted as she mounted the stairs, envisioning that shadowy figure from the window waiting for her at the top. Every third step creaked. She cursed.

The hallway was clear. Now running, she hustled into the guest room and flung open the closet. The mirror vibrated from the force of her haste. She smashed in the code to the safe, ready to pull the door open, plant the organs, and leave.

Red light.

No, no, no, she thought to herself in a panic. She tried again, hoping she had just mistyped. It remained locked.

She reached for her phone from her back pocket and dialed Chris. "She changed the combination for the safe. It won't open. I don't know what to do."

He cursed in turn, trying to think of a new plan. "Can you put the bag in her fridge?"

"I can, but she will see it right away, and she will know. She'll probably just put it back in my fridge," Addison stammered. A door slammed shut on the first floor. She jumped, then held her breath.

"Someone's in the house," Addison whispered, closing and locking the guest room door as quietly as possible. She struggled to take a deep breath.

Chris pulled back the curtain. "Her car is still gone."

"Maybe she parked somewhere else? Someone is in here." Addison's heart thrashed against her chest.

"You gotta get out of there. Forget about the organs; just leave them there," Chris demanded.

"I can't. I have to at least hide them." She quieted her voice even more midsentence as she heard footsteps climbing the stairs. Step, step, *creak*.

Looking around the room, she couldn't find a good hiding spot, for herself or the organs. There was no more time. She ran for the window and slid it open. Behind her, the door handle jiggled, softly at first, then with ferocity.

Addison kicked out the screen, then sat on the windowsill with one leg out, resting her foot on the small portion of roof that covered the porch below. She set the bag down on the shingles. The organs and blood pressed against the side of the opaque bag, hinting at what was hidden inside. Suddenly, a wood-splitting crash sent a tall man surging into the room, shoulder first.

Fear gripped Addison as she looked at him. He was dressed head to toe in black, wearing dress shoes and a ribbed turtleneck. His short black hair was slicked back. Sunken-in eyes so brown they were almost black stared straight into her soul. There was an emptiness in him. His lips were small and sharp, curling back to reveal gritted teeth. His nose was misshapen, like it had been broken before. There was something familiar about him, Addison realized. He had the likeness of someone in the photo of the Oz Music Club. Franklin, she thought. But it couldn't be. This man looked like he was in his forties—strong, tall, and vivacious.

Turning her head, she ejected the rest of her body from the window, but the bottom of her pant leg caught on a jagged part of the window frame. She lay flat on the roof with her right leg angled at the window, her foot still inside.

"I've got you," the man grumbled, reaching for her foot.

She tugged and thrashed with all of her might. His hand tightened against her shoe. The bag of organs began to roll down the roof. A muscle in Addison's back pulled as she reflexively reached for the bag. It came to a stop mere feet before tumbling from the edge. She groaned. Sharp pain set in, and exhaustion made her want to give up, but she didn't. One more powerful kick released her with an audible tear. The man fell backward with her shoe in his hand.

Scrambling, she pulled herself up to her knees and crawled toward the bag, snatching it up. There were only two options: up or down. Climbing higher to the top level of the roof, she searched frantically for a spot to dispose of the organs. To her left, the redbrick chimney. That could work, she thought. Maybe the organs would just get stuck midway and no one would ever find them. Although they also could just fall all the way down and Mrs. Wells would find them easily.

Addison swallowed, feeling the magnetic energy of someone coming up behind her. Glancing back, she caught sight of a black figure approaching the edge of the roof.

Trying to maintain her balance, she trekked toward the right back side of the roof. Her foot caught on a loose shingle, jolting her forward. Like a surfer catching a wave, she caught her balance, and the shingle hurtled to the ground.

"You have nowhere to go," the man quipped, now on the same level as her. Due to his size, each step had to be plotted carefully.

A ravenous bark garnered Addison's attention. The neighbor just behind Mrs. Wells's house had two Rottweilers, Moe and Curly. She only knew this because they were always breaking loose and running around the neighborhood. Four times she had returned them to their owner, a grumpy old man with a retired sense of humor.

More shingles scraped free and tumbled behind her. Clothes rustled, and the man grunted with each misstep. Gripping the handles of the bag, she brought her arm back. Getting into position, she readied herself to pitch the bag to the dogs like a baseball player. It careened into the air, soaring in the right direction, but began falling too soon. Addison's eyes grew big, and she held her breath as the bag tapped the top of the fence. It bounced off, the weight of it tilting it toward Mrs. Wells's side.

Moe jumped like a show dog, spit wicking from his jowls. He caught the bag with a snort as his body bounced off the fence and fell into the dirt. Moe flung himself off his back, and together the dogs tore the bag to shreds. Their sharp teeth sank into the organs, and they ate every last piece.

Unsure of where to go next, Addison turned to face the man.

"Franklin," she shouted.

The man stopped, now only a couple of feet away. "Franklin is my father."

"Who are you, then?" she asked, searching for a way out in her periphery.

He sneered, hands outstretched, ready to grab her. Ready to choke her out of existence. She darted, stepping lightly. She maintained her balance while she prayed that her feet would touch only the secured shingles. He followed, inevitably finding the loose shingles. Just before she could step down to the lower roof, a hand grabbed her shirt, pulling her backward.

Together they fell. The impact knocked the wind out of her. Blood dripped down her cheek.

"Get away from me," she commanded, fighting back. Gaining some distance, she descended to the lower level.

He followed. Remembering there was a trellis at the far end of the roof, she darted toward it.

"Hurry," Chris yelled, standing in the driveway with his car keys in hand.

The man raced to stop Addison, almost succeeding. A group of loose shingles caught his foot like a trap, and he slipped onto his back. When Addison's feet hit the ground, the man rolled down onto the lawn with a thud.

Gaining composure, Addison rushed forward, watching Chris climb into his car. The roar of the revving engine empowered her.

With a violent groan, the man pulled himself to his feet and marched with increasing speed toward Addison. She hobbled into the street, coughing and wheezing as she tried to catch her breath. Like a mallet, her racing heart relentlessly pounded against her rib cage.

A disheveled Addison clamored for the door handle. She could hear Chris hitting the unlock button repeatedly, then the lock button once she was inside. There was no time for them to put on their seat belts.

The car slid backward down the driveway, whipping into the street just inches from crashing into the man, who thrust his arms outward to brace himself on the trunk. Acceleration pressed them into their seats as Chris stomped his foot on the gas. Soon the man was just a speck in the mirror. Seconds later, he was gone.

TWENTY-THREE
ADDISON

AN OPEN VISOR offered Addison a view of herself. Her hair was tangled. Black mascara had smudged around her eyes. Dried streams of blood trailed down her cheek from a cut on her temple. Her tired hands rested in her lap, still snug inside a clean pair of nitrile gloves. Warily, she looked at Chris. Her eyes welled up; his squinted with fury.

They each made several attempts to find words. Any words. But it wasn't until they reached the apartment complex and pulled into Chris's parking space that the silence broke.

"Who the hell was that? Is that the guy you saw in the window?" Chris groaned.

"I think so. He's the son of Franklin Edwards," Addison explained. "Franklin was mentioned in some of those news articles from my dad's fishing shack. A premed student from Redlands, Maine."

"So I guess he took on the family business. What did

you do with the stuff?" Chris turned off the engine and shifted his body toward Addison.

"I threw it over the fence to the yard behind hers," Addison said. Chris stared back blankly.

Addison continued, "That's the house where Moe and Curly live. The Rottweilers."

"Oh." His tone lifted as he nodded. "What did they do?"

"They tore everything up and ate it." Addison squirmed at the thought.

"Honestly, that was a pretty good idea," Chris admitted.

"Yeah, in the moment, but now we don't have that evidence anymore if we need it." Addison ripped off the gloves and balled them up.

Sighing, Chris replied, "You're right. It's okay—I think it's for the best right now, until we can figure out what we're going to do next."

"What about the kitchen? The blood in my refrigerator? We still need to go back and clean." Addison felt her eyes widen.

"I cleaned it as good as I could while you were across the street. I'm sure there are still micro traces of something, but nothing too noticeable. I wrapped everything into itself within the plastic and put it in another grocery bag from Mrs. Wells. It's in the trunk."

"Did you wear gloves?"

"Of course I did."

Addison breathed a breath of relief. "Okay, so where

do we go from here? We're not safe at my house, and they probably know where you live by now too."

"What about Veronica's?" Chris suggested.

"We could go there, but she lives so close to Mrs. Wells. I don't want to lead them there, especially so soon after what just happened. I don't want her to get killed because of me. These people are murderers—we don't need her on their radar too."

"Let's grab some clothes and all of your dad's stuff from my apartment, then drive to a random hotel for tonight until we think of something else. We can get rid of the bag on our way."

Addison approved of Chris's proposal, though when they arrived at his complex, she insisted it would be faster if she ran up alone to grab everything.

It took them five minutes to pack everything in one black hard-shell suitcase, which Addison lugged over to the car and tossed into the back seat.

"Listen to this," Chris said, turning the volume knob as she climbed back into the passenger seat. A man's commanding voice filled the car.

"The victims of the gruesome Rusty Tavern murders have been identified as mother and daughter Jane and Celine Waterford," the man said, enunciating each word with precision before discussing the case briefly.

"Oh my gosh," Addison exclaimed, receiving a look of equal astonishment from Chris.

"Why would they kill Jack's wife and kid when he was part of the cult?" Chris wondered. He backed out of the parking spot and began driving again.

"Maybe his wife threatened to expose them. She must have known something they didn't want her to know for her to be silenced like that," Addison replied while pulling up Facebook on her phone.

She searched for Jane Waterford, finding a profile that matched the location and age. All her page had to offer was endless Candy Crush Saga and Bejeweled Blitz posts, dog videos, and sparkly "Happy Holidays" graphics. Nothing informative.

Celine Waterford did not have a Facebook account, but she was on Instagram, which Addison discovered after confirming Celine's age and appearance. A Google search of her name found her in an article titled "Most Creative Nail Artists in Maine" along with a link to her Instagram profile. To Addison's surprise, she had ten thousand followers. Quite a following for a girl in a small town.

Gel-X nails were her specialty, and her artistic designs garnered thousands of likes. Pop art and neon appeared to be her areas of expertise. Addison felt inclined to screenshot a couple of the designs as nail inspiration, even though she seldom got her nails done. She always kept them short for work, and her anxiety caused her to become an occasional nail-biter.

Four rows down on Celine's profile, Addison noticed a hand that looked familiar.

"Ronnie got her nails done by Celine?" she exclaimed.

"Seriously?" Chris asked, looking over at the photo of Veronica's brown hand with its long square nails that had a cartoonlike appearance, painted as they were in a deep-red matte polish and framed in black. White details had been added to give the illusion of light reflecting off the surface. Addison remembered seeing her best friend with those nails recently. Veronica bragged about how good her nail lady was whenever she'd come back with a new set, which Addison would unfailingly compliment.

"It seems a little weird," Addison said, "but it doesn't surprise me that Ronnie would go to someone this popular and talented, especially if she is local."

"It's a little weird, but how many nail artists like this do you think work out here? Veronica strikes me as the kind of woman that would only go to the best."

"True. I wonder if she knows yet," Addison said, imagining Veronica's reaction to the news.

"You should ask her about Celine. Maybe she knows something that can help us figure out why they killed her."

"That's a good idea. I can also catch her up on everything that's happened," Addison said.

"I don't think you should tell her *everything*." Chris shot Addison a look of concern.

"She is my best friend," Addison protested.

"Yes, I know. But I really think the brain-and-heart situation should be left out. It's better if no one knows about that. If it somehow comes back on us, we can get in big trouble for tampering with evidence or something," Chris warned. "Not to mention, we don't want to put her in danger. You said that yourself."

Addison agreed, then dialed Veronica's number.

Chris continued to drive west in search of a motel, frequently glancing in the mirrors for any unwanted followers.

"Hey, babe," Veronica answered with excitement.

"Hey, I have a question for you." Addison got straight to the point. "What was your nail lady's name?"

"Celine. Why? Oooh, are you thinking of getting your nails done finally? 'Cause she is the best. I want to help pick the design, though," Veronica asked with a giddiness that told Addison she hadn't yet heard about what happened.

"No, I just needed to confirm that was your nail lady before I tell you what I just heard on the radio." Addison looked to Chris, unsure of how to break the news to her friend. "I'm so sorry, Ronnie, but Celine was just identified as one of the women found dead at the Rusty Tavern."

Silence.

"Are you okay?" Addison asked solemnly.

"Yeah," Veronica replied sluggishly. "This is terrible."

By the sound of her voice, Addison wasn't sure if she was more upset about Celine's death or the loss of an amazing nail person.

"I wanted to ask you, did she ever talk to you about stuff?" Addison began. "Like, her life?"

"A little bit, yeah. Where is this going, Addy?" Veronica asked softly.

"I think whoever's after me, the Darkside of the Rainbow people, are the ones that killed her and her mom. I'm not sure if you knew anything about her family, but her dad was Jack Waterford, the guy who chased me and died in the car crash and also happened to be the nurse who coded my patient with me." A breath. "The same Jack that cofounded Darkside of the Rainbow with Mrs. Wells. It's all connected. Celine and her mom must have known something, or maybe they were going to expose something," Addison explained.

"What makes you think this secret society or cult or whatever it is are the ones that killed them?" Veronica inquired, her voice becoming rigid.

"First of all, Unknown texted me about the murder with some cryptic *Wizard of Oz* text. I'll send you a screenshot later if you want. Secondly, they had pyramids drawn on their foreheads in chalk, just like . . ." Addison slowed her speech. "Just like they did to my mom when she was fifteen."

"Wow," Veronica said. "I mean, that's pretty convincing. What are the cops saying?"

"I don't know; they haven't really released many statements. They definitely aren't talking about Darkside of the Rainbow. At this point, I doubt they even know who that is," Addison replied. "But back to Celine—did she ever say anything that seemed odd, like she was talking about Darkside? Or anything about her parents?"

"Not really." Veronica gathered her thoughts. "She lived alone in a studio apartment downtown. Oh, she did have a cat named Leaf. He's one of those huge Maine coons. Don't ask me why she named him Leaf; he was orange and white with amber-colored eyes. She was kind of weird like that, though. She gave everything weird nicknames—I was Pomp-adorable; her nail drill was Dizzy; there was one other really weird one . . . oh yeah, her car was Bits or Bitsy. Besides that, she never really talked about her family, at least nothing that I can remember off the top of my head. I'm sorry, Addy, it was always just small talk."

"It's okay." Addison sighed. "I don't even know if it would make much of a difference, finding out what she or her mom knew. I already know it's connected."

"I really don't want to talk about her anymore right now," Veronica sniffled.

"I'm sorry," Addison said.

"Have you been back home yet?"

"Yeah, this morning, and someone definitely was in there," Addison answered.

"How do you know that? Was the door busted?"

Addison hesitated for a moment. "No; actually, the lock was fine—it's like whoever broke in had a key or something. My parents' bedroom door was open, but I am positive it was closed when I left that night. And the photo of my dad was missing from their dresser."

"That's so scary, Addy. Have you been staying with Chris?"

"Yes, I'm with him now," Addison replied.

"Oh good, tell him I said hi." Veronica's voice was tinted with jealousy.

"He says hi back."

"Are you guys at his place right now?"

"No, actually, we're going on a little getaway for the night," Addison said. "With everything that's been happening, we just felt like a change of scenery would be nice."

"Cute," Veronica honeyed. "Well, let me know when you get there safely."

"I will," Addison promised.

The call ended. Guns N' Roses' "Appetite for Destruction" blasted through the speakers from start to finish. Once they reached a point where there had been no one else on the road for miles, they pulled off into a rural area to dispose of the plastic waste from the trunk. In the cover of trees, they began a controlled burn to destroy the evidence before getting back on the road. Addison felt a wave of discomfort. Could it really be that easy?

They pulled into a little one-story motel. Spanish architecture with arches, columns, and clay roof tiles gave the place charm. Vacancy flickered in blue neon light, hanging just below a weathered *King's Inn Motel* sign. It was missing the letter *M* and, by the looks of it, was on the verge of missing a few more. On the canvas of an evening sky, long clouds bled pink and orange until the blackness pushed it all away.

Parking was in the back, a feature that had prompted them to choose that motel. From what they could see on Google Maps' street view, it offered more discretion than most others. That, and it had three stars instead of two.

With a beep, Chris locked the car and slipped his crutches beneath his arms. Addison wheeled the suitcase into the lobby. It smelled like a Vegas casino, cigarette smoke and cleaning products unsuccessfully masked by a pleasant fragrance—cucumber, melon, and rose. White walls housed framed prints of knights and swords, a theme that carried throughout the rest of the motel. The carpet must have been fifty years old. It was thick and brown, worn down in places from where people had lingered too long. Behind a light-blue Formica counter was a thin old man who peered up at them from behind a copy of *Outdoorsmen* and square-framed glasses that were too big for his face. His beady eyes glanced at them, then darted back to his magazine.

"How can I help you?" he asked in a rich, clear voice.

"We need a room, just for tonight," Chris said.

"And in the back, away from the street if possible," Addison added.

The man peered over the magazine at Addison, looking her up and down. "Ninety-eight dollars. Checkout is at eleven." Flipping the magazine over to save his spot, he dug into a drawer for a pair of keys. "Room twenty-seven." He tossed them onto the counter.

Addison and Chris stood there for a moment, expecting him to ask for more information, but he didn't. A hundred-dollar bill had been placed on the counter in exchange for a key covered with questionable black grime. Addison was sure he thought she was a hooker.

Their room was on the back side of the motel, as requested, granting them a direct view of their car. The cold blast of the air conditioner greeted them as they entered their room, locking every lock behind them. The curtain rings scraped against the metal rod as Addison tugged the drapes shut.

Chris flung the suitcase onto the king bed, which was covered in white sheets and a blue bedspread with frayed edges. Dark-wood nightstands stood guard on either side of the bed, and a matching dresser held a thirty-two-inch off-brand flat-screen.

Addison unzipped the suitcase and retrieved the leather satchel, dumping all of its contents onto the bed. She put the key, book, and cassette tape to one side and gathered the papers in a stack to the other.

"I'm really hoping the missing pages from the book are in here." Addison climbed onto the bed to sit in front of the papers. "If not, they probably burned along with the shack. Without those pages, I can't finish decoding the clue."

Chris joined her on the bed, moving the news clippings they'd already read to a new pile. "There's got to be something that can help us in here," he said. "What have you decoded so far?"

"'Key opens,'" she replied.

"Check this out." Chris handed Addison a hand-written note that had been stapled to court papers.

Franklin Edwards was the reason they all moved to Maine after Paul died. He was born in Redlands originally but left to California for college. Because of him and his influence on the group, my life was forever changed. Hannah and I would have never met. Sometimes I wish we hadn't.

Our souls were not satisfied when we were together, and our souls were not satisfied when we were apart. It was toxic and exciting. Scary at times. We created life together. That was the best thing either of us had ever done. We had plans for our future, for Addison's future. Darkside had other plans. The bitter cost of loving her.

Franklin became a neurosurgeon and opened his own practice in Maine. He married a much younger, impressionable woman who was lured into the cult, just like Hannah. They had a son, Alex, who became a surgeon as well, but he specialized in cardiothoracic surgery. Like father, like son. He lost his license after a big malpractice lawsuit in 2006.

"I think we found out who was removing the organs," Chris said.

"And who was chasing me on the roof," Addison added.

It's a shame he didn't lose it sooner. There were three different claims. Information on each can be found attached. The first claim was that he left surgical instruments inside of six patients, which led to severe complications. The second claim was from a woman who said she went in for a valve replacement surgery, but when she came out she was missing her right kidney. The final claim was that he operated under the influence of drugs or alcohol. He never ended up doing jail time, but he did have to pay a large sum of money in settlements, and he ultimately lost his license to practice medicine.

I know they chose to come to Maine because of Franklin, but I couldn't get Hannah to tell me the real reason they all had to move in the first place. They were on top of the world in California. They had members in the local police department. Members on the board of education. A recording studio. Record label. Money. Mansions. I knew there had to be a reason they left everything behind. I think the reason was Lacy Brown.

TWENTY-FOUR
LACY BROWN

CALIFORNIA, 1979

Whenever I find myself in a less-than-desirable situation, I sing my favorite song—"I Will Survive" by Gloria Gaynor. Today was one of those days. I'd be lying if I said I don't like California—the beaches, the weather, and the tans are all very desirable—but I loved my life back in Dallas, Texas. If my dad had been offered what he calls the opportunity of a lifetime just one year later, I wouldn't have been forced to relocate right in the middle of my senior year, class of '79. Unfortunately, he was offered a tenured position teaching law at UC Berkeley five months ago, and instead of graduating with my friends, I just graduated with a bunch of strangers.

My father has been grooming me to become an attorney since I was four years old. Instead of Barbies, he bought me a briefcase, and instead of playing tea party, I was encouraged to defend my stuffed animals in a make-believe court. My mom would secretly tell me I could be whatever I wanted to be when I grew up—even a famous singer. But she died from leukemia when I was ten, and so did my dreams of creating my own future.

Today, I am supposed to meet with a counselor at UC Berkeley to go over my admission to their school of law.

"Wear something . . . professional," my father shouts as he fills his thermos with coffee and runs out the door. He is always in a hurry yet always arrives early. His first class doesn't even start for another hour, and we live two minutes away from campus.

I pretend not to hear him. He may dictate my career path, but I will not let him dictate how I dress. I run upstairs to finish getting ready. A long sleeveless dress with buttons and dark-colored stripes accentuates my athletic body. It is modest but still shows off my hard-earned tan and toned arms. I choose a thick belt with rhinestone detailing to cinch my waist. On my feet, I wear brown leather platform heels that have a studious appeal. How's that for professionalism?

Running into the bathroom, I check the mirror. My hair is a dark shade of brown, almost black, and layered to my shoulders. I have bangs that naturally swoosh to each side. A few swipes of mascara to each eye and some brown-red lipstick is all I do for makeup. Pressing my lips together, I make sure the lipstick is even, then I smile to check my teeth. My eyes are devoured by my smiling cheeks. Cheeks that everyone says they'd kill to have, but I'd consider killing not to.

Now I'm at the school, waiting for Frances to invite me into her office. As I bounce my crossed leg, I can't help but think this is a waste of time. Between my dad being a professor here and my grades, my admission is guaranteed. But, as my father says, "there are some technicalities that can't be avoided." Apparently, that means meeting with a counselor and getting a tour from a senior student.

"Come in, dear," Frances says, waving me over from the doorway.

I sit in her office. Her desk is in the center of a wood-paneled room with dark carpeting and dim lighting.

"Let's begin," she says, smiling from behind half-rimmed glasses. "I understand your father is Professor Brown." She sifts through folders. "And that makes you Lacy Brown. Here you are." She opens a folder and skims through. I assume she is pretending to read my file.

"So you want to be a lawyer like your father," she remarks. "Those are some big shoes to fill."

I want to say no, *he* wants me to be a lawyer, but I know that wouldn't be professional.

"Yes," I say with a thin smile.

"Everything looks great. Impressive grades." She nods. "I will just need a couple of signatures from you. While you go over that, I'll grab you a copy of your class schedule and a list of books you'll need to buy." She walks away.

I sign everything without reading anything, then receive my papers.

"I thought I was going to be interviewed," I say.

"Would you like to be interviewed?" she asks.

"No," I admit, and offer a grateful smile.

She laughs uncomfortably. "All right, dear, well, that's all I need from you. If you wait out in the lobby, Jane is going to show you around campus. She is a brilliant student and a wonderful musician."

"Musician?" I ask, perking up.

"Yes, she even has a band, though I forgot the name." She ushers me toward the door and shuts it once I'm out.

Before I can sit, Jane walks in. I stare at her in awe and surprise. If she isn't famous, I'll be in disbelief. She has the air of a movie star, one who has already accepted so many Oscars that the next would become a paperweight—that is, if she even remembers to take it home. Blonde hair flows down her back, bangles jingle on her arms, and we are wearing the same dress. Her energy is like a vortex; it pulls me in so strongly I could be swallowed whole.

"Lacy?" she asks, her eyes twinkling.

"Yes, you must be Jane," I say, shaking her hand. I'm quickly pulled in for a hug after she remarks that we are "twins," and we start walking out of the admissions building.

"Frances tells me you're a musician," I say.

"As a matter of fact, I am," she says, smiling. "I sing and play piano."

"That's stellar," I enthuse.

"Do you play any instruments?"

"Not exactly," I say. "I do really enjoy singing for fun, though."

"Lacy, that counts as an instrument." She locks arms with me. "Sing something for me."

"Oh, I don't know." I hesitate.

"Come on," she encourages.

I begin singing "I Will Survive," but my voice cracks from the nerves.

She sings the next line. Her voice is rich and smooth. Before I know it, we're belting out the chorus together.

Just like that, we've formed a bond. She is everything I want to be and everything I once dreamed of becoming. It's probably a good thing she's graduating this year, because if I get too close to her, I might drop out of law school and pursue a singing career.

"These are the dorms," she says as the tour continues. "That is Paul's dorm, if you ever want to get high." Her laugh is both feminine and contagious.

Paul emerges just as we're about to move on to the next building. The breeze catches his scent—vanilla and cannabis. As I look him up and down, I find myself wanting to get high for the first time.

"Wow," he says after locking his door. Light-wash jeans hug his muscular legs.

"I'm Lacy," I say, shaking his hand.

"She sings," Jane announces with excitement.

"Does she?" He smiles at me with a smile so beautiful it could kill me.

"Are y'all in a band together?" I ask, cringing at my use of *y'all*. I've been working hard to adopt the California accent, but sometimes the twang works its way out.

"Where are you from?" Paul asks, giving me more attention.

"Texas."

He and Jane shoot each other a look, like they have an inside joke I just reminded them of.

"What?" I refuse to pretend I didn't catch it.

"Oh, nothing," Paul says.

"Paul has a thing for girls from the South," Jane reveals. My crush for him grows stronger. I can feel it in my stomach. Butterflies.

"Where are you girls headed?" Paul changes the subject.

"I'm giving her a tour of the campus," Jane replies.

"That will take you forever. Just give her the map and come with me."

My heart is pounding. I want to know where he's going.

"I can't do that to her. I like her too much to rob her of a real tour." Jane locks arms with me again.

"Oh, it's really okay." I smile. "A map will be fine. Besides, most of my classes are at the school of law, and I've already been there before."

"All right, if you say so. I'll make sure to get a map to you," Jane promises.

"Excellent." Paul walks in front of us. His scent catches in the wind, once more filling my nostrils. It smells good enough to get me high all on its own. We follow him to his 1977 Pontiac Firebird, glossy black with a gold firebird on the front and gold rims. He must have modified it some, because it seemed to have extra wings and scoops that made it look faster and more expensive. He opens the passenger door for me, but before I slide in, I look over to Jane.

"I'll meet up with you guys soon, okay? I have to grab something back at the house. Also, I'll grab that map for you before I forget," Jane says, already walking backward. Momentarily I feel my stomach turn with unease, but Paul is so cute and such a gentlemen that I will it away and wave goodbye to her. Perhaps this day isn't going to be as boring and mundane as I initially expected.

"Where are we going?" I ask.

"You'll see," he teases, and turns on the radio, which I abruptly turn off.

"Seriously." My tone is more stern than I intended.

"I am going to take you to lunch, if you'll let me, because Lord knows Jane is going to take at least an hour to meet up."

"And after lunch?"

"After lunch, we are going to the studio to record a couple tracks. I can drop you off at home if you aren't comfortable," Paul explains.

"No, no, I want to go, I just . . . I really like you guys, but I don't really *know* you."

"Let me fix that." He grins. "I'm Paul. I play guitar in a band called Breathe. I'm majoring in music theory. I love music of all kinds, though my favorite band is Pink Floyd. I'm an only child, born and raised in California. Your turn—tell me about you."

"Me?" I ask, knowing I'm not remotely as interesting as him or his friends. "As you know, I'm Lacy. I moved here from Texas this past year with my dad for his job. I love singing; my favorite artist is Gloria Gaynor. I'm planning to become an attorney."

"Would you like to sing on one of our tracks?"

That one question makes me melt like a bar of chocolate on a hot summer day. Jane and Paul have managed to eliminate any reservations and regrets I had about moving to California in a matter of hours. In fact, now I'm starting to believe this is exactly where I am supposed to be. My mom would be proud. Maybe I can achieve my father's dreams for me concurrently with my own.

We go to a cute and expensive lunch in the marina amid clear blue skies and gently bobbing boats. I feel underdressed, but Paul assures me I look beautiful. We share a clam chowder bowl, and he buys me my first lobster tail; color me impressed. I'm sure we will be late to the recording studio, because after paying the bill, he takes me for a walk around the marina. The air is salty. Seals bark in the distance. He holds my hand like it's our fourth date, and at the perfect moment, while leaning against the railing overlooking the ocean, he pulls me close and presses his lips against mine. Best first kiss ever, though I don't dare tell him I've never been kissed before.

At three o'clock, we arrive at a discreet black building with all the doors and windows blacked out. We walk inside and down a hallway into the studio, where a group of musicians berate us for being late.

"Paul will be Paul," Jane says, smiling from atop a barstool.

Everyone is at their respective instruments, and once Paul ducks under his guitar strap, he offers introductions.

"That's Yessenia on bass, Hannah on tambourine, Franklin on drums, and you know Jane on vocals and piano." He turns toward a glass window that runs the length of the room. "Over there operating the controls is Jack and George." Everyone waves when introduced. Jack is kind and quickly sets up a chair for me inside. It looks exactly as I imagined a recording studio to look: high-end equipment, red carpeting, black foam walls.

"Let's start with 'Gamble.'" Jane speaks into the microphone. The song is upbeat and complex, full of harmonies. My favorite of the three tracks they record is titled 'Scars of the Past,' probably because that's the one they let me sing on. It's a slow song with a beautiful piano melody. Paul is the main vocalist on the track and I sing backup, harmonizing on the chorus.

Scars of the past (of the past)
Are reminders of just how fast (how fast)
Our love had come to be
Scars of the past (of the past)
Place holders of a love that lasts (that lasts)
True love no one could ever believe

Time is passing so quickly it's already past midnight. Their instruments are put away, and just when I think we are going to leave, Franklin pulls out a joint. I am having so much fun I don't want the night to end, so I join in, not knowing what to expect. I find the more I smoke, the happier I feel. Laughter fills the room. Paul tugs me into his arms as we all sit on the floor in a circle. He plants little kisses on my head, squeezing his arms tighter around my waist.

"All right, all right, now let's get to the good stuff," Jack says.

"The good stuff?" I ask.

"LSD," Hannah offers, exchanging a look with Paul. I catch her looking at him again when he places a small square with a picture of a four-leaf clover onto my tongue. He licks his finger after, then places one on his own tongue. I can feel her eyes on me when we kiss. The squares dissolve on our dancing tongues, and I'm swept into a state of weightlessness.

"Have you ever played with a Ouija board?" Jane asks me.

"No, isn't that what you use to communicate with ghosts?"

They laugh at me.

"I guess you can consider him a ghost," Jane says as she leaves the room. Jack follows, and minutes later they return in black cloaks with a Ouija board and candles.

"Him?" I ask.

"Lights," Jane whispers. Hannah and Yessenia jump up and turn off all the lights in the studio while Jane and Jack proceed to ignite several candles around the room. Part of me feels uneasy, but Paul squeezes me tighter, giving me several soft kisses on the cheek.

When the girls return from turning out the lights, they too are wearing black robes. They all join back into a circle with the Ouija board in the center of the floor.

"Just me and you." Jane grabs my hand, pulling me out of Paul's arms and into the middle of the circle with her. I resist for a moment. She drags my hand onto the planchette, then places her fingers on the other side.

"Divine, guide us, let us receive your message." Jane's eyes are closed. "We found the girl from Texas."

The speakers crackle on, and a song starts playing. It's "I Will Survive" by Gloria Gaynor. I look around to see who put the track on. Paul is missing from the circle. He must be trying to make me feel more at ease. At least that's what I think until I hear an earsplitting screech and the song begins to play in reverse.

Our hands are sliding across the board. I know I'm not moving mine, but I assume Jane must be moving hers. I don't believe in ghosts.

K-I-L-L T-H-E V-I-R-G-I-N

Gasping, I pull my hands away. Eyes are on me, burning through me everywhere I look. My heart is racing. A wave of nausea presses at my stomach. What seemed like a joke is now beginning to feel real. A sense of impending doom blossoms. I stand up to run, but everything looks as though it's moving. Someone grabs me from behind, but I can't turn to see who it is. They are crushing me. Laughter echoes.

The song continues to play in reverse while Jane approaches me with a long black candle. She blows out the flame, then draws something on my head with ashen fingers. Everyone's face is becoming distorted. I see their skin melting from the bone like paint dripping from canvas. I must be hallucinating.

I'm being tossed around, but I can't maintain my balance. My head slams against Paul's guitar as I fall to the ground. The strings rattle. Just as I clamor to get my footing, someone kicks me in the back. I fall back to the floor. Another kick jolts my entire body. Paul's face looks down at me in rage. Flames engulf his eyes. The corners of his mouth continue to turn up higher and higher in a way that isn't anatomically possible.

"Kill the virgin," Paul growls as he lifts me back to my feet, holding me steady. Jane lunges at me with a dagger, digging it into my flesh and ripping it out with a splash of blood. I scream but am quickly silenced by Paul's firm hand. My teeth sink into his finger, only enraging him more. He holds me tighter, wrapping an arm around my throat. I fight to find a breath of air. Jane stabs at me again with another volley. Bile drips from my abdomen, mixing with my blood, and my vision goes black.

TWENTY-FIVE
ADDISON

IN THE MESS of articles and journal entries, Addison uncovered the missing book pages. Her eyes looked to the sky in praise. Flipping through the book, she slipped them into their rightful places, then picked up where she had left off. She was careful not to lose count as she unveiled each precious letter.

Key opens my work locker. Find the factory number twenty three.

"Where is his old work?" Chris asked.

"The Miller factory," Addison said.

"From the photo," they said in unison. Was that why Unknown had taken it?

"That's the one in Carter City. The one they closed down," Addison said.

Ping. She reached for her phone.

UNKNOWN

I see you're not in Kansas anymore. You
can run, but you can't hide. Not queen,
not duke, not prince. King.

"How do they know we're here? They must have followed us," Addison's vision tunneled. Thoughts raced in her mind. Was she being watched everywhere she went? Were there cameras in the room?

"Hey, look at me," Chris said, recognizing Addison's panic. "Slow, deep breaths."

Tightness squeezed at her chest as blood pounded in her ears.

"Imagine yourself in a boat on the ocean." Chris gripped her shoulders, forcing her to face him. "Close your eyes. Now envision yourself on a boat. There's a massive storm, rain is flooding the deck, waves are thrashing against the sides. Picture a black, angry sky."

Addison struggled to take a deep breath but homed in on the visual.

"Now, with your mind, make the storm go away. Starting with the rain." A beat. "Now focus on the waves. Use your mind to calm them. They're slowing down. The sun is starting to shine through. Focus on pushing the clouds away to reveal a calm, blue sky."

It was working. As she pictured the storm leaving, so did her chest tightness, freeing her to take a breath. Chris continued to guide her through meditation until her panic attack completely subsided.

Addison fell into his arms. "My anxiety has been getting so much worse lately."

"It's okay, Addy, there's a lot going on." Chris combed her hair with his fingers. "I know I can't take it away completely, but I'll do everything I can to help you through it. As far as the text goes, we're safe inside a locked room. If someone did follow us, I will protect you, and we'll call the cops."

Addison let out a deep breath. "Okay, that makes me feel a little bit better."

Chris moved everything off the bed, then lay beside her, pulling her closer to his warm body. Tender lips kissed her forehead, then each eyelid, and her lips. A satisfied breath escaped her. She tugged his shirt over his head, running her fingers over every muscle on his stomach before releasing his pants. Releasing him. Her top glided upward in his hungry grip, catching on her breasts for a moment before they dropped with a gentle bounce. Their bare chests collided. They kissed as though their tongues were dripping with honey, catching and savoring each invisible drop.

She felt the weight of his body on top of her. It was comforting. Beneath him, she shimmied her panties down before turning him over and climbing on top. Her breath caught for a moment as he slipped inside her. Sweat dripped from their bodies as he pumped harder to maintain rhythm when she grew tired. His hands slipped from her hips as he clamored to hold on. He gripped tighter and tighter, his fingers digging into her skin. Deeper. Harder. But the pain was soon forgotten as they reached crescendo and their bodies relaxed.

TWENTY-SIX
ADDISON

DECEMBER 5, 2024

Morning swept in, and with it came several brief trips to the window in search of something or someone out of the ordinary. Unknown. Visions of a shadowy figure hunched between cars, spying and waiting to pounce, intruded Addison's mind, but she stopped herself, forcing the image to dissipate and aligning her thoughts with the exhilaration of having decoded the hidden clue. Excitement morphed into abbreviated passion between questionable sheets.

After getting cleaned up, they packed everything back into the suitcase. Per their mutual decision, Addison tore up the cipher into tiny pieces, flushing some down the toilet and tucking the rest into an empty potato chip bag destined for the garbage. It also seemed like the best idea to dispose of the decoded message in the same manner, as it was already ingrained in their minds. As for the book, Addison couldn't bring herself to destroy it, at least not yet.

Checkout was at 10:55. With five minutes to spare, they grabbed complimentary coffees and bagels from the continental breakfast the motel worker had failed to mention at check-in. Though the coffee was hardly palatable, they needed the caffeine.

Carter City was east of Redlands, in the exact opposite direction from the motel. To get to the Miller factory, they would have to return home first, or at least pass nearby.

"I'm going to buy a gun beforehand, just in case," Chris said, gripping the gearshift.

"I think that's a good idea," Addison replied. "Can you drop me off at Veronica's while you do that?"

"It's safer if we stay together."

"I know, and I agree, but I want to at least let her know what's going on first. While I'm there, I can stash the satchel in her room so at least that stuff will be safe."

"I don't love that plan," Chris cautioned, "but if you really feel it's best, then I'll drop you off at her place."

"I do," Addison said reaching over to hold his hand.

ADDISON

Ronnie, I'm going to stop by in a couple hours

VERONICA

Yay! I can't wait to see you.

———

Chris's car idled in Veronica's driveway long enough to facilitate a farewell kiss. A spread of fruit, cheese, and crackers awaited Addison on the kitchen counter when she entered Ronnie's house. Anything Veronica prepared, no matter how simple, looked like it was styled for a cookbook. A variety of artisan cheeses snaked through perfect clumps of grapes, sliced strawberries, and plump blackberries. Dried flowers and herbs garnished the platter to give it a decorative appeal.

"I know I say this all the time, but you really need to make an e-book or something," Addison said, stuffing a pile of cracker, cheese, and blackberry into her mouth.

Veronica giggled. "I'm glad you like it, I'm trying some new cheeses." She sat on the barstool beside Addison and popped a grape into her mouth. "How was your little getaway with Chris?"

"It was really good. The motel was a little run-down, but cute in its own way. We were able to get a more secluded room. Unknown still knew where I was." Addison swiped to her messages and showed Veronica.

"That's so creepy, Addison," Veronica said. "When is all of this going to end? I don't understand why you haven't called the police yet. I'm worried you're going to get hurt."

"I know, but everything will be okay. Chris is getting us guns for protection. We won't let anything happen to you either," Addison swore. "Also, I finished decoding the hidden message in the book, so all of this should end soon, once I find what my dad was hiding." Addison shoveled another cracker into her mouth. Veronica swept up the crumbs with her hand.

"What did the message say?" Veronica enthused.

"It said that the key opens his old work locker," Addison revealed.

"Do you know where he used to work?"

"Yeah, the Miller factory in Carter City. It closed down probably fifteen years ago now."

"When do you plan on going?"

"As soon as possible. Well, once we have the gun." Addison swiveled to look at Veronica.

"Wow, you really figured it out, huh," Veronica said softly. "Promise me you'll be careful and call me if anything happens."

"I promise," Addison said. "Guess what else? I found evidence that links Darkside to the Rusty Tavern murders." She paraphrased what she'd found online.

"I wonder if it was Alex who removed the heart and brain? Wasn't his dad the surgeon you told me about?" Veronica put the pieces together.

Addison felt her heart palpitate. She couldn't remember if she'd specified which organs had been removed. Had she even told Ronnie about Franklin Edwards?

She'd likely mentioned these details in one of their conversations, she reasoned, or perhaps Veronica had done research of her own on the Rusty Tavern murders. After all, the only way Addison and Chris knew about the organs being removed was from what they'd learned in online forums. That and what they'd found in the refrigerator.

"Are you okay?" Veronica asked after an awkward silence.

"Yeah, sorry, I was just thinking about everything and how crazy it all is. I just can't believe I'm wrapped up in this," Addison covered, crafting another cracker with cheese.

"I know. It feels like a movie or something, like something you watch but never expect to happen to you in real life," Veronica said before ushering Addison upstairs to her room.

Veronica unfolded red lace underwear and red silk pajamas from her top drawer to change into. "I'm going to take a shower real quick; let's talk more after. Make yourself comfortable."

"I will," Addison said, hopping onto the bed under the neon pink glow of LED strip lights that lined the perimeter of the ceiling. Veronica never used the big lights. Every room in her house was either dimly lit with lamps or glowed pink and red from neon signs and strip lighting.

Once the bathroom door shut, Addison pulled out her phone. She realized she had never messaged Unknown back and decided it was a good time.

ADDISON

Since you seem to be so good at tracking me, where am I now?

On the black dresser directly across from the foot of

the bed, Veronica's phone screen lit up. Addison's head reared backward. *It couldn't be,* she thought to herself.

ADDISON

Hello?

The screen lit up again. Heart racing, Addison waited for the screech of the shower handle and the sound of water hitting the tile floor. Gently, Addison slid to the edge of the bed and, with ninja-like stealth, tiptoed over to the dresser. Without touching the phone, Addison glanced at the lock screen, which was still illuminated.

NOTIFICATION FROM DISCREETCOMM

New message from Addison

Her eyes grew so wide they almost burst. Scooping up the phone, Addison began attempting to unlock it—888888 didn't work; neither did 000000 or 123456. She tried Veronica's birthday, but that didn't work either. She had to get it on the next try or else she'd be locked out. Deep inhale. Long exhale. Her gut told her to try the numbers for RONNIE—766643. *Fitting,* she thought as she typed the sixes. The lock symbol opened and she was in.

Addison opened the DiscreetComm app. Tapping on her name, she uncovered all the messages between her and Unknown, confirming without a doubt that Veronica was her mystery messenger. Her posture stiffened with the sting of betrayal. She pushed down her emotions, just like she would at work. There would be plenty of time to cry about it later, but right now she needed to focus.

Backing out of the app, Addison opened Veronica's text messages. The top conversation was between her and Tye.

> **VERONICA**
>
> I can't wait to see you again, I'm so glad I stole you.

> **TYE**
>
> I'm glad too, sexy.

A shampoo bottle crashed to the floor, bouncing to a stop. Addison jumped quickly, closing the app.

"Are you okay?" Addison yelled, adding curses under her breath.

"I'm good," Veronica shouted back.

Deep inhale, long exhale. Ronnie typically took long showers, but Addison knew she had to be fast.

The next conversation was between Veronica and Mrs. Wells, who was saved as "Jane T."

> **VERONICA**
>
> I think she is getting close to finding out what he was hiding.

> **JANE T.**
>
> Good, keep her close, get her to tell you everything. Is the recording device still in her living room?

> **VERONICA**
>
> Yes, but she rarely is down there. We'll have better luck with me just trying to get her to talk.

JANE T.

Do you think we will be able to convince
her to join?

VERONICA

I don't know, she seems to think a lot
more like her dad. It might be too risky.
Her desire to remain loyal to him as her
patient is sickening too. I think right now
our best bet is beating her to whatever
he was hiding, then we can deal with
her later.

JANE T.

What a shame. I really adore that girl,
but if she tries to expose us we can't
hesitate to do to her what you and Alex
did to Jack's girls.

VERONICA

She just called me, she is going to come
over. I'll make sure to get the key
tonight.

JANE T.

Perfect. Accomplish this and you will
earn the much deserved title of Grand
Magistrate. Don't mess this up. Alex will
be on standby.

Addison's anxiety turned into blood-boiling anger. Her stomach churned with disgust. All the feelings from the betrayal with Tye came rushing back. The texts rendered her unforgivable.

Water splashed against the shower tiles, which muffled Veronica's singing. She belted out the lyrics to the Beatles' "Lucy in the Sky With Diamonds." Her pitch was perfect.

Addison knew she didn't have time to scroll all the way to the top of the message stream. Instead ,she went back to see what other messages she could find. Celine!

CELINE

Can we just talk about this?

VERONICA

No, there's nothing else to say. You're heartless. You knew your mom was planning to expose our Geminid Meteor Shower ritual on December 13, something you and I have been working hard on for months to gain our titles, but you didn't even care enough to warn me. Your mom's little anonymous tip to the police cost us this ritual that could have helped make us millionaires and probably has cost me the title of Grand Magistrate.

CELINE

She's still my mom. I literally just lost my dad, she's all I have left.

VERONICA

That right there is why you aren't worthy of being in Darkside. WE should be your family. Your loyalty should be to US. You're just as weak and flaky as your dad.

CELINE

My dad CREATED Darkside. You wouldn't even have this opportunity without him. We can still do the ritual, we can figure out another location

Jane created Darkside. Your dad was just lucky enough to be there when it happened.

No, Celine, we can't. You've ruined it. Consider yourself expired.

TWENTY-SEVEN

ADDISON

THE WATER SHUT OFF. Addison fumbled with Veronica's phone, causing it to fall. Dropping to the floor, she quickly scooped it up off the carpet, closed all the apps, and put it back where she'd found it.

"Everything okay?" Veronica yelled.

"Yeah, I just dropped my phone by accident," Addison lied, tiptoeing back to the bed.

A gust of steam spilled into the room, making Veronica's entrance like that of a rock star. The moist heat quickly cooled, and the fog vanished slowly from the bathroom mirror. Ronnie's long black hair was secured to the top of her head in a towel, her body clothed in crimson. The scent of cherry blossoms and jasmine filled the air as Veronica finished rubbing Love Spell lotion into her legs. It had been her signature scent since middle school.

"Let's paint our toes like we used to," Veronica said, plopping herself next to Addison, who suddenly felt like a slob.

"We'll have to start doing that more often now that your nail lady is dead." Addison couldn't help herself.

Veronica's eyes narrowed, then subtly shifted toward her phone. Addison caught it in her periphery.

"Sorry, that was a little insensitive. I'm down to paint our nails; you pick the color," she said.

"I think you should pick," Veronica countered. "They're under the bathroom sink."

Addison sauntered into the bathroom. Behind her, Veronica shuffled over to her phone at the same time. Addison squatted down and began to rustle through the nail polish bottles with one hand while opening her text messages to Chris in the other. Using her body, she shielded her phone.

ADDISON

V Unknown

"Did you find a color?" Veronica inquired from the doorway.

Addison jumped. "You scared me." She pulled out whatever polish her hand had landed on. Lime green. She stood up, slipping her phone into her back pocket.

"You scare easily," Veronica teased as she grabbed the polish from Addison's hand. "Some people say life is more bearable with a bit of courage." She beat the bottle against her palm.

"Who says that?" Addison asked with a searing glare. "The Cowardly Lion?"

Veronica let out a lighthearted laugh while setting up a spot on the floor for them to do their nails, tossing pink toe separators, wooden cuticle sticks, and cotton balls into the area. From her desk drawer she retrieved two *Cosmopolitan* magazines covered in old dried nail polish like a Jackson Pollock—old polish from the last time they'd done their nails together as teenagers. Addison received her magazine, which said "100 Love Questions" in bold letters, a quiz she vaguely remembered taking, and slipped it beneath her feet to protect the carpet.

"I thought you'd pick a darker color," Veronica said, shaking the bottle. Little did she know Addison hated the idea of lime-green nails just as much as she did, especially during the fall season.

"I just wanted to try something funky and different," Addison replied as she shimmied the toe separators between her toes.

"I'll do you first," Veronica said, pulling Addison's right foot closer. A little too hard.

"How is everything going with Tye?" Addison asked.

"Amazing, actually. We had a little getaway of our own last night. He surprised me with a date at that cute little Golden Girls–themed Airbnb that we've always talked about staying at. Of course, I told him how much I love that show. He made this whole amazing candlelight dinner. Lobster tail and arugula salad. Surprisingly, he is a good cook"—she laughed—"but the house had every season of *Golden Girls* on VHS, so we popped that in, had a little *Golden Girls* marathon, then made our way to the hot tub to . . . you know." The corner of her mouth flicked upward along with her left brow in a flirtatious smirk.

"Wow, I can't believe you stayed there without me." Addison feigned jealousy, a feeling she would definitely be experiencing if she hadn't just learned who the real Veronica was.

"I know, I'm sorry." Veronica made a pouty face. "But we will go soon, I promise."

"We better." Addison retrieved the bottle of nail polish. "Okay, your turn."

Veronica scooted closer so her feet were right in front of Addison and hugged her knees.

"Oh, by the way"—Addison pulled together every ounce of courage in her body—"I texted Unknown while you were in the shower."

Veronica released her knees, eyes darting to meet Addison's. Fear melded into scrutiny as they both searched each other, trying to discern one another's true emotions.

"What did you say?" Veronica looked back down at her toes as Addison worked her way to the final two.

"I asked why they put the organs in my fridge, and I told them I planted them inside Jane's house." Addison misled with a trap.

"I thought the dogs ate them?" Veronica's face registered instant regret.

"Aha," Addison shouted, the magazine crinkling beneath her feet as she shot up. "I never even told you that the organs were ever in my fridge, let alone what happened to them."

Veronica rose to her level. "Of course you told me." She clambered for an excuse. "You've been going through a lot of stress; you must have forgotten."

"Don't even try to gaslight me, Veronica. There are only two ways you would know about that." Addison began backing toward the door. "Either you're sleeping with Chris and he told you, or you are Unknown. Since I know Chris would never touch *you*"—the words erupted from her mouth with a condescending inflection—"it must be the latter. You are Unknown." Addison pointed an accusatory finger at Veronica.

"Shows how much of a real friend you are. You promised to tell me everything, but instead you told Chris." Veronica sneered, her eyes burning with madness. "And I wouldn't let Chris touch me even if he wanted to." She rolled her eyes. "It wasn't your phone that fell while I was in the shower, was it? It was mine, you little snoop." She stomped toward Addison on her heels, careful not to smudge her nail polish.

"Yes, Veronica, you're right, I was looking in your phone, because when I texted Unknown, I saw *your* phone light up. I sent a second message, because I thought there was no way my best friend would pull something so conniving and evil. But it lit up again. So yes, I did look. And I found out who you really are." Addison's hand was now on the door.

"And who am I?" Veronica taunted, positioning herself to lunge.

"You are the Tin Man," Addison spat. "A heartless bitch."

Ronnie laughed, her cheeks raising as if she found pleasure in that title. "And you are the coward."

"You know what? You did do one thing for me, in the vein of your cult and cryptic sayings. 'I never would have found my courage if it weren't for you.'" She quoted *The Wizard of Oz*.

While Veronica had her attention on her phone, probably sending a message to Alex or Jane or some other cult member Addison hadn't yet met, she twisted the doorknob and bolted down the stairs. Unlike Veronica, Addison couldn't care less if her nail polish got messed up. And it did. Lime-green polish smeared against the carpeting on the stairs and smudged on her skin. Once she was at the bottom, she ripped the toe separators from her feet, tossing them at Veronica.

"Get back here," Veronica cursed at Addison as she descended the steps, shrieking when her pinkie toe rubbed against the bottom stair. "You are going to pay for this," she growled, leaping toward Addison. Together they fell against the tiled floor with a thud just feet from the front door.

"I've already paid for it," Addison said through gritted teeth as she wrestled. "I paid for it with our friendship."

"You think you're so wise," Veronica snarled, gripping a chunk of Addison's hair in her hand and ripping at it. "I can't wait to taste your blood."

Addison thrust her knee into Veronica's abdomen as hard as she could, forcing Ronnie to release her grip. Now hunched over, Veronica gasped for air while

Addison rubbed the pain from her head, fully expecting to see blood on her hand. It was dry. She flung the door open, but just before she could step out, Ronnie launched at her. They tussled onto the front porch, biting and kicking. Veronica made several attempts to hit Addison in the face, but only one blow was successful. It was, however, a strong enough blow to draw blood from Addison's bottom lip. She felt it start to swell and pulse.

"Addy," Chris yelled from an open window as his car bounced into the driveway. He ripped off his seat belt and flung the door open, cocking his gun and pointing it at Veronica. Addison whipped around and pummeled Veronica in the face with a ceramic lawn ornament. Under different circumstances, Addison would have laughed at the irony of hitting Veronica in the face with a garden gnome that was holding up its middle finger. Poetic justice. Veronica was subdued long enough for Addison to run over to the passenger's side of Chris's car and jump in.

From the lawn, Veronica spewed curse words and violent grunts, then quickly ran back into the house for her car keys. It didn't take long before she caught up to them, tailing closely behind in her car.

TWENTY-EIGHT

ADDISON

DECEMBER 5, 2024

DARKNESS ENGULFED THEM, only the faint yellow glow of an occasional streetlight offering a reminder that something else, anything else existed. Chris maintained a fast but reasonable pace within city limits, which enabled Veronica to tail closely behind. But a sharp, unexpected turn caused her to miss hitting a man crossing a crosswalk with his dog by a narrow margin. He pumped his fist in anger.

Edging toward the old highway, Veronica pressed her foot deeper into the pedal, taunting Chris. Her front bumper sped into his back taillight, sending bits of crushed plastic into the street, some of which snapped beneath her back tires.

Enraged, Chris twisted his grip tighter against the wheel. Leather crunched. His veins bulged from his forearms as the speedometer climbed—ninety, ninety-five, a hundred.

"Careful, Chris." Addison reached for something to

grab on to, bracing herself. Veronica matched his energy, pushing her car to its limit. Everything outside passed by in a blur.

"Where are we going?" Addison asked as her hand settled into the overhead grab handle.

"We're ending this now. I'm driving us to the factory. We are going to find what your dad was hiding and finish this once and for all." Determination settled into his brows.

"But what about Veronica?" Addison asked.

"She already knows anyway, right? We kind of don't have a choice. If we don't go now, they will for sure get to it first."

Chris was right, and Addison knew it. Her mind raced as she realized how her anxiety had blinded her from seeing the truth. The reason Unknown knew where she was at all times was because she shared her location with Veronica. The reason her front door wasn't tampered with or damaged was because Veronica had a spare key. The reason Darkside would get to the stuff was because Addison had revealed the hidden message that she'd spent hours decoding to Veronica. Each thought enraged her more. She encouraged Chris to drive harder, faster. To do whatever it took to lose Veronica.

Memory told Addison they were nearing Carter City. Chris slowed the car momentarily as they drove through town. Cruising down Main Street, they passed angled parking spots and charming old buildings with protruding window displays. Snow had collected in the corners of some window panes like a Hallmark movie. At the end of the row was the local sheriff's office. The shallow glow of a desk lamp reflected through the opaque glaze of the front window.

Veronica wasn't as careful. With great risk, she swung her car onto the wrong side of the road, enabling her to pull up beside Chris and Addison. With their windows lined up, Veronica scowled at Chris. Taunted them.

"She's insane," Chris shouted, picking up speed as soon as he'd left the sheriff's office in their wake.

Veronica veered to her right in a dangerous game of cat and mouse. Chris swerved before she could make contact.

"Hold on," Chris said, prompting Addison to grip the overhead grab bar again. As they gained speed, the already dark night became even darker beneath the shade of ash trees that lined either side of the road for miles. Branches hung overhead, blocking out much of the sky. Veronica continued to drive on the wrong side of the road, violently honking her horn.

"What the hell is she doing?" Addison squealed, peering over Chris.

"I don't know. She's going to get herself killed."

"Don't say that."

Buzz, buzz. Addison's phone began to vibrate. It was Mrs. Wells. Addison panicked. She wasn't ready for that confrontation.

"Answer it," Chris said, reading the contact name. "Let's see what she has to say."

"Hello," Addison said.

"Hi, honey, it's Mrs. Wells." The older woman's voice was calm and soft. Sweet.

"You mean Jane," Addison retorted.

"It doesn't have to be like that, honey. You could put a stop to this right now. Think of your friendship with Veronica. Do you really want to throw all of that away over something so silly?"

"I didn't throw anything away. She did. She's the one that betrayed me on multiple levels. If you guys wanted me to join your cult so badly, why have you never asked? You've just been keeping all of this a secret from me this whole time?" The words spewed from her mouth like sparks.

"We are all you have left, honey. We wanted to tell you everything a long time ago, but your mother kept getting in the way," Mrs. Wells began.

"My mom left when I was a teenager. You've had like ten years to tell me," Addison said, cutting her off.

"No, dear, your mom never really left. She stayed close, always sticking her nose where it didn't belong." Mrs. Wells's voice became sour. "Somehow she and your father reunited and started working together, trying to stop us, though we didn't know it was him until this year. As you know after snooping in my safe, Hannah led me to believe he was already dead." She paused for a moment. "They kept interrupting our rituals, costing us precious time and money. We had a meeting with Hannah to try to come to an agreement. After everything we'd been through, we owed it to her to give her a chance to live. She promised to leave us alone if we promised not to include you or invite you to join us, so we agreed. Then, this year we found out she had been working with Andrew all along. He was supposed to be dead. That bastard cost us more than I can even begin to explain. Franklin tried to stop him, shot him even, but he fought back and killed Franklin."

"What happened to my mom?" Addison asked.

"Oh, she is dead now, honey. When she was starting to convince Jack to leave Darkside, I knew she needed to be dealt with once and for all. She wormed her way in by becoming best friends with his ditzy wife," Mrs. Wells explained. "But now none of them are a problem anymore." She laughed in a way Addison had never heard her laugh before. A howl wicked enough to darken any room.

"You are evil." Addison's voice shook.

"Oh, sweetheart, I am not the evil one," she honeyed.

"When did you get Veronica to join?"

"Don't you know who her mother is?" Mrs. Wells questioned.

"Obviously. Yessenia," Addison said.

"Yessenia what?"

"Yessenia Gonzales," Addison said in a matter-of-fact tone.

"No, Yessenia Velasquez." Just as Mrs. Wells said it, Addison realized what she was getting at. Veronica's mom was in that photo of the Oz Music Club, though she had been over one hundred pounds heavier then. Unrecognizable. Ronnie's mom had been in Darkside all along.

"Did you guys plan for Veronica and me to meet

too?" Addison fought back tears. "Was this all just a play in your evil game?"

Mrs. Wells chuckled. "No, when you guys met it was purely by chance. We couldn't have planned it better if we tried."

"How long has Veronica been involved in Darkside?"

"Eighteen is the age of initiation," Mrs. Wells explained, "but for her, just like your mother, we made an exception because she too was special. She was officially inducted on her seventeenth birthday. So, yes, honey, your friendship did start out as a real friendship. There were no ulterior motives on her part. But the divine wants what the divine wants, and she had to obey."

Suddenly, Addison screamed, blinded by the headlights of a truck driving toward them at full speed. "Veronica!" She dropped her phone to the floorboard. Chris honked several times, slowing down as much as he could. Ronnie didn't waver but kept pressing forward, trying to keep up with them. Her eyes weren't on the road—they were locked on Chris and Addison. The horn wailed. Whoever was driving the truck was just as distracted.

Chris rolled his window down. "Veronica," he screamed. "Stop." His hand flailed to warn her.

Addison saw Veronica shifting her head toward the road. She finally saw the truck coming. Color drained from her face. A quick jerk to the steering wheel caused her to swerve at the last second, but she wasn't fast enough. The large, heavy-duty truck crashed into her fender. Her car spun out and slammed hood first into a tree trunk.

With a deafening screech, Chris slammed on the brakes. His car shook to an abrupt stop. The truck slowed for a moment, as if to contemplate whether or not to stop, then sped away with minimal damage. Addison bolted from the passenger's side, leaving the door agape. Darkness clawed at her periphery, squeezing her vision narrower and narrower until all she could see was Veronica's mangled BMW.

TWENTY-NINE
ADDISON

SHARDS OF GLASS blanketed the ground, crunching beneath Addison's feet as she pulled the driver's door open. Squinting in the darkness, she fought to see the state of her friend. Ex-friend. She didn't even know what to consider Veronica anymore. But she didn't want to consider her dead.

One headlight still glowed, illuminating the trunk of a thick ash tree that had become one with the hood of the car. Steam and smoke snaked through the light. Once Addison's eyes adjusted, she saw a deployed airbag spattered in garnet. Veronica was hunched over, the seat belt holding her in place. Streams of blood seemed to come from everywhere.

"Ronnie," Addison wailed, patting her face gently at first, then with more force. No response. She quickly scanned Veronica's body; no overt signs of fracture or obvious penetrating objects. Her fingers traveled up

Veronica's neck, which was now sticky with blood, and felt for the carotid artery. No pulse.

Addison's heart raced and her breath quickened as she reached into Veronica's pants for a femoral pulse. Nothing. The seat belt hissed free. She caught Veronica's limp body with a grunt, almost losing her balance, and dragged her to a flat surface. Chris hurried over to help clear debris out of the way with his crutch as he held his phone out as a flashlight.

"Come on, Ronnie," Addison shouted as she placed overlapped hands atop Veronica's chest. As she began compressions, she felt ribs snap beneath her palms, cracking loud enough to make Chris wince.

"One, two, three, four, five . . ." Addison counted aloud to thirty before tilting her jaw back and giving two manual breaths.

"Should I call an ambulance?" Chris asked. He already had the number pad pulled up on his phone.

"No," Addison shouted through huffs, maintaining an internal count. "Come on, Veronica, come back."

Chris paced. "I don't know what to do. We can't stay here."

Addison stopped after the second cycle of compressions to check for a pulse. Nothing. She let out a scream. Tears dripped from her nose. She noticed the edge of Veronica's phone poking out of her front pocket.

"Here." She tossed it to Chris. "It's 766643."

He unlocked the phone, awaiting more orders while Addison resumed compressions.

"Call 911 from her phone." Addison fought to get the

words out. Her arms burned. Her knees bled from pressing into the shards of broken glass. Blood stained her hands. "Wait, check if she told anyone about the factory first."

Chris complied, verbalizing to Addison what he found. Jane and Alex had both been notified of the locker in a group text. He mentioned that all the other messages had been sent prior to Veronica finding out.

"Nine-one-one, what's your emergency?" a feminine voice asked in a modulated tone.

"There's been a bad accident off the main road in Carter City along the Alley of the Ashes," Chris said.

"Sir, what is your name?"

He remained silent.

"Sir?" the woman repeated.

Chris placed the phone in Veronica's open palm, still connected to the operator.

"We have to go," he whispered, ripping Addison from Veronica's chest. For a moment, she fought him with what little energy she had left. As much as she hated Veronica in that moment, it killed her to give up. But it didn't take long for her to succumb to his grip. Glass scraped beneath their shoes as they hurried back to his car.

Tears continued to pour down Addison's face in a fit of rage and sadness until there were no more tears to cry. Dirt and blood stained her clothes. She had been a nurse long enough to know it wasn't her fault that Veronica died, yet she also knew no amount of time or experience could diminish the grief of giving everything you had to save a life and still failing. Terrorized by the sorrow of losing her best friend that night, both in life and in death, Addison's eyes burned. Red and blue lights flashed in the rearview mirror. Addison kept watching until distance and darkness blotted them out.

Chris placed his hand on Addison's thigh. A gentle touch. He granted her the silence she needed to gain her composure. Five minutes was all it took.

"Who should we expect to run into when we get there?" she asked.

"Jane and Alex, at least, though we probably will arrive first. Veronica had also called Tye. It was a short phone call, so whatever she told him was concise."

"Tye has probably been in the cult this entire time," Addison blurted out. "They probably used him to try to lure me in."

Chris shrugged. "At this point, nothing would surprise me."

As they turned right down a long, bumpy dirt road, the only light came from their car. An eerie fog crept low to the ground, swirling with the dust that the tires kicked up. Soon the dirt road became a gravel road, then a poorly paved road, and the old factory came into view.

Most of the red-painted letters that had once spelled MILLER were now chipped and faded. Though it was obvious the building had been abandoned, the concrete infrastructure stood strong. An overgrown parking lot riddled with cracks and weeds offered them a spot right up front.

"Looks like we beat them," Addison said, searching the lot for other cars.

"Unless they parked somewhere more hidden."

"Should we?" Addison looked around, observing everything the headlights illuminated.

"I honestly don't think it would matter at this point. They know we're coming."

Chris stopped Addison before she could exit the car. "Wait, we need to go over a few things." He retrieved a Glock 17 from the glove box and handed it to her. "This one is yours."

She released the magazine, looking to confirm that it was fully loaded, then slammed it back in with her palm. Chris smirked, releasing a breathy laugh. On their second date, he had taken her to a shooting range, where she had demonstrated her aptitude for wielding and shooting a gun. He had told her how attractive it was watching her handle the weapon. While they both enjoyed shooting, this was the first time they'd ever felt a desire to own a gun. Or a need to.

"Here are some extra bullets, just in case," Chris said, handing her a small bag of 9mm rounds.

"What about yours?"

"I have one too." He lifted his shirt and pulled a pistol from his waistband. Addison worked to conceal an emerging smile. She hadn't seen him slip it in there.

"Should we come up with a plan or just wing it?" Addison asked.

"Neither of us have been here before, so I guess let's just wing it. We should stick together unless for some reason splitting up increases our chances of survival, so we could save each other or something." Chris's own smile faltered. "But I really don't want to split up unless it's absolutely necessary."

Addison nodded in agreement.

"Do you think it will come down to that?" Her brows knit together.

"I hope not, but knowing who we're dealing with, we can't take any chances."

Addison gripped the locker key tightly before tucking it into her pocket. With the gun secured in her grasp, she and Chris walked toward the factory.

THIRTY
ADDISON

A PAIR of dilapidated doors with glass-paneled windows hung from their hinges. Thick chains welded the long brass door handles together, helping to prevent the doors from falling. On either side, floor-to-ceiling glass windows had been smashed in and partially boarded up. Chris jabbed at the window to the left with a crutch, knocking down the remainder of the glass and wood to grant them entry.

The air smelled of wheat and mildew. Both cell phone flashlights had been activated, illuminating dancing particles of dust. Papers were scattered about the floor and chunks of linoleum tiles were lifted or missing.

They approached a U-shaped reception counter. A green rotary phone, which Addison discovered still had a dial tone, sat next to a directory. Chris started flipping through it.

"There has to be a map here somewhere." Addison sifted through papers and rummaged through drawers.

"I found the number for the staff lounge," Chris said. "Based on the extension, it seems like it's on the first floor."

"Here." Addison stacked a trifold paper on top of the directory and flattened it out. "A map of the factory."

Outside, a car door slammed. Chris and Addison ducked, snuffing out their flashlights. Addison's pulse quickened, and she could almost hear Chris's pounding heartbeat.

"Did you hear one door or two?" Addison whispered.

"I don't know; it was hard to tell," Chris said. "Hurry, this way." He led Addison toward a hallway on the left, putting more pressure than he should on his bad leg but enabling them to move faster.

"Are we even going the right way?"

"I'm not sure, but we need to get somewhere safe to check the map." Chris lowered his voice even more at the sound of falling and crunching glass. Whoever it was, they were inside now.

At the end of the hallway, there was a split. Without giving it too much thought, they darted to the right and then to the left, making their way deeper into the factory. Addison took a mental note of each turn.

"In here," Chris whispered, holding a door open for her, then gently guiding the door shut. They turned their flashlights back to full brightness.

Finding themselves in a conference room, they laid out the map on a large oval table. After a brief argument, they determined they were in conference room B.

"Okay, we aren't too far off," Chris said, pointing to

the staff lounge on the map. He dragged his finger across, denoting the path. "We just need to get down to the end of this hallway, turn left, go all the way down, and then it should be the last door on the right."

"That's not too far," Addison began, but was abruptly squelched by Chris's hand. Footsteps shuffled outside in the hall. Addison carefully turned the phones over, blocking the light against the table. They listened carefully, scared to even swallow for fear it would give them away. The feet scuffled a moment longer, then faded into the distance.

Addison let out a breath. "What if they're just waiting for us at the end of the hall?"

"It's possible, but I guess we have to risk it," Chris said. "Keep the flashlight as dim as possible and have your gun ready."

He peered out first, then Addison. Once her eyes adjusted to the darkness, she could make out shapes. Paper on the floor. Loose linoleum tiles stacked on top of each other. Doorways. Filing cabinets and boxes. Like a SWAT team, they sneaked into the hall, guns pointed, using only one dim flashlight to guide their way.

At the end of the hall, they plastered their backs against the wall. This time, Addison peered first—clear. They moved toward the left into a heavily cluttered hallway. It was like a maze. They maneuvered around boxes, beer bottles, old magazine racks, and other Miller paraphernalia. Occasionally, the crutch would bump into a box and they would pray no one heard it.

Addison felt uneasy. She fully expected someone to

jump out at them every time they passed a doorway or a tall stack of boxes. The more she thought about it, the more she could almost see it, an illusion of her mind. Her stomach churned as they reached the end of the hall.

Chris grabbed her wrist to guide the light up toward the door. *Staff Lounge.* "We're here," he said, gripping the doorknob and pushing inward.

"Help me move this," Addison said. They dragged a dusty brown couch in front of the door. Without a lock, they needed the extra security. If nothing else, it would allow them enough warning to prepare.

"I wonder if there's still power?" Chris said, trying the light switches. No such luck. With a few taps, he increased the flashlight on his phone back to full brightness. Addison did the same.

The cushions on the leather couch that now blocked the door were worn down. The couch had been situated next to a square oak coffee table littered with magazines. A side table fashioned from a stack of boxes housed a dead plant in a terra-cotta pot. In one corner was a kitchenette with gray or maybe light-blue Formica countertops, an industrial coffeemaker with three burners, a microwave, and a full-sized refrigerator. Along the walls were a couple of mismatched tables and chairs. On the wall hung a clock with the Miller High Life girl wearing a red dress and sitting on a crescent moon. It had stopped at three fifteen.

"No lockers," Addison pointed out as she sifted through the magazines. A *Hustler* issue was nestled between several *MAD* and *Life* magazines.

"Over here." Chris gestured. Through a small corridor, they discovered another room. Dirty coveralls were piled on the floor, while still others hung from the edges of open lockers.

"Do you see any numbers?" Addison asked as she shined the light up and down. It looked like a gym locker room. Two long benches spanned the middle of the room, and yellow lockers lined the four surrounding walls.

"Not yet. Most of them are missing or too damaged to read. What number are we looking for again?"

"Twenty-three," she replied.

"Well, this one says twenty-eight," he said, brushing dust away with his finger. "It must be along this row."

Addison ran over, first trying the key five lockers to the left of twenty-eight. The key slid in but wouldn't turn. She tugged at the door, trying the latch, but it wouldn't open. Next she tried five lockers to the right of twenty-eight. The key slid in. After a deep inhale, she turned the key. It opened.

"I'm in," Addison enthused, releasing her breath. Her stomach tickled with butterflies. Mostly from nerves.

Chris hobbled to her side, leaning his crutches against the next locker over and shining the light inside for Addison to see.

"Wow." Addison stared, unsure of what to look at first.

"What is it?"

"It looks like a ton of evidence against Darkside," Addison said, sifting through countless cassette tapes labeled with names of different members. There were a couple of unlabeled VHS tapes, an envelope with handwritten letters, legal documents, and contracts with bloody fingerprints. In another envelope were photos of the members of Darkside next to what Addison assumed —based on the writing on the back—were victims of their ritualistic murders. There were two zip drives on the top shelf. Addison tucked one into her pants pocket and tossed the other to Chris.

"How are we going to carry all of this?" Addison asked as she looked around for a bag.

"Let's check if any of these lockers are open. Maybe we can find something inside," Chris suggested.

One by one, they tugged on the doors. Light illuminated the insides, revealing a few possible vessels, mostly lunch pails, though they were too small to carry everything. Chris stumbled upon a gym bag. Time seemed to have amplified the smell of sweat and dirty socks. He held his breath as he dumped out old sneakers, shorts, and a protein bar well past its expiration date.

"Here." He offered the bag to Addison, holding it open.

She began shoveling everything inside.

"Did you hear that?" Chris whispered, causing Addison to pause for a moment. They pressed their flashlights against their thighs as they listened. The doorknob to the staff lounge rattled. Someone was trying to get in. Addison hurried, scooping the last of the evidence into the duffel bag and zipping it up.

The rattling became more vigorous before going completely silent. Had whoever it was given up?

Suddenly, a body slammed into the door at full force, shifting the couch slightly.

Addison threw the bag over her shoulder in cross-body fashion, then lifted her pistol to the door. "Where do we go?"

"There's no other way out. Just stay calm and quiet," Chris said, standing next to Addison with his gun drawn as they used their phone flashlights in lieu of mounted lights.

Another slam. The couch shifted. And another, harder this time. The couch shifted even more. After three more forceful impacts, the couch moved just enough for someone to slip through.

Step after step, a tall dark figure lugged closer to them until he stood in the middle of the staff lounge, panting. Close enough for target identification.

"Tye." Addison said.

THIRTY-ONE

ADDISON

"BACK UP, or I'll shoot you," Addison shouted with her hands pressed firmly against the gun. Her grip was steady.

"Don't shoot," Tye said, holding his hands up.

"Back up," Addison yelled with even more force. "I should have known you were part of Darkside. All that weird stuff that kept happening every time I was with you. The song playing in reverse at Careless Whisper and again at Rusty Tavern. Then you seduce Veronica. You guys were probably dating the entire time."

"Whoa." Tye held up his hands. "I am not part of Darkside of the Rainbow. And Veronica and I are not dating."

"You clearly know who they are. Is this part of your initiation? Following us and trying to stop us?" Addison adjusted her grip. "And don't even try to lie to me about Veronica. I saw you kiss her. She told me everything."

"No, I am not trying to join them; I am trying to stop

them. Whatever you saw or heard regarding me and Veronica is not based in reality." Tye reached down toward his belt.

"Stop," Addison yelled. "I will shoot you."

Tye lifted his hand back up. "I am with the FBI, if you'll let me show you my badge you'll see."

"I don't trust him," Chris interjected. "This is probably part of their plan to trick us so we hand over the evidence; then they destroy it and kill us."

"Look, I get it, I wouldn't trust me either if I was in your position, but I'm telling you the truth," Tye said. "You can search me yourself."

Addison cautiously approached him. Both guns remained locked on the target. Addison reached toward his belt and retrieved a folded wallet with a badge inside: *Tye Howard, FBI.*

"It looks legit, but you could have just made a fake one."

"Whatever Andrew was hiding in the locker, you can give to me. I will take it in, and we can put an end to all of this," Tye said, reaching toward Addison's bag.

"No." She pulled away forcefully. "Absolutely not. You've lost all my trust. No one is turning this stuff in but me."

"Understood," Tye said.

"If you really are FBI, was all of this part of your investigation? Casablanca? Tricking me into dating you?" Addison pressed.

"Yes," Tye replied. "The FBI has been watching Jane Thatcher for quite some time now. I know it was wrong and I'm sorry, but when I found you on Casablanca and discovered you were her neighbor, I used it as a way to get inside. Then I found out Hannah was your mother, and I knew it was imperative to get close. When you introduced me to Veronica, I did more research into her background and learned she was the daughter of Yessenia, another alleged member of the cult. I needed to explore that link deeper."

"What even tipped the FBI off in the first place? They were killing people in the seventies without ever getting caught."

"Lacy Brown," he said. "They got sloppy with her murder. They overlooked who her father was. About a year ago, I was tasked with reviewing cases that had gone cold. This one intrigued me, so I worked toward piecing everything together. Looking for mishandled evidence. We came so close to pinning the murder of Lacy Brown on Jane; I just needed to gather a little more information. We received an anonymous tip that Jane was actually a member of a cult called Darkside of the Rainbow. We had a meeting scheduled to go over everything with the anonymous tipper, but he never showed."

"Because Franklin shot him," Addison finished.

"And he ultimately died in the hospital, which you know." Tye's voice trailed off. "We discovered this later."

"So, let's turn everything in," Addison said. "You go first, and we'll meet you at the sheriff's office."

Overhead speakers crackled on. A factorywide sound system had been activated. *Tap, tap, tap.* The sound of a finger against a microphone.

"Testing," a voice graveled with a feedback screech. It was familiar and rough. *Alex,* Addison thought.

"Give me that," another voice ordered. "This is Jane. I would like to formally welcome you to tonight's event." She unleashed a sinister laugh.

"After your little *lunch* break, do join us in the Brewhouse Courtyard for a little party. Addison, honey, you've been more trouble to me than you're worth, but it will soon be over. You'll be joining your mother in the grave." The sound of sand trickling rang out through the speakers. "I've just turned over the hourglass. Listen closely. That's how much longer you've got to be alive. And it isn't long, my pretty."

Wicked laughter ensued but was soon concealed by the scratch of a record and a subsequent song. "Revolution 9. »

Addison shuddered.

"Come on, we have to get out of here," Tye ordered. Chris and Addison allowed him to draw his own gun but maintained their stance against giving him the evidence. Together they moved the couch and crept back into the hall.

"Revolution 9" was creepy enough on its own, but it became even more ominous against the backdrop of a dimly lit abandoned factory with cultists on the loose.

Retracing their steps, Addison and Chris worked their way back toward the front of the building, Tye keeping pace. As they were about to round the corner to the hallway that contained conference room B, a wall of smoke billowed toward them, stinging their eyes. They coughed, tugging their shirts up over their noses. Flames raged at the far end of the hallway, threatening to come toward them.

"We have to find another way," Tye said with a cough.

There was only one other direction to go from where they stood. Pressing on and flinching with every falling box and snapping tile, they found themselves being led strategically like cows to the slaughter. Corridors had been blocked off or set ablaze. Doors were locked. The path had been chosen for them, and it led directly to the courtyard.

"We should have split up a while back," Addison said.

"They would have just killed us faster," Chris said.

"We are going to have to face them," Tye admitted. "Whether we want to or not, the courtyard is the only way out at this point. Once we're out there, we can find a way back to the cars. It's our only chance." He turned toward Addison. "You're going to have to run to the car while we distract them. You have to get the evidence out of here safely."

"I'm not leaving Chris behind," she implored.

"Addy, you have to. We can't let them win," Chris said sternly.

Black smoke nudged them into the courtyard, which was paved in gray stone with overgrown hedges. Weeds protruded from every crack. In the center of the courtyard was a large water fountain. Still, murky water swirled with plant debris. On the ground, right in front of the fountain, were three spray-painted red *X*'s. Directly behind the middle *X* sat a large wooden hourglass. Sand continued to slip through the crevice.

"Welcome." Jane's voice came back over the speaker system. "Take your places."

"I'm not standing there," Addison said, loud enough for Chris and Tye to hear.

"Time is running out," Jane announced, emphasizing the word *time*. Another record scratch echoed through the courtyard, and the song "Time" by Pink Floyd began playing.

Clocks chimed overhead, a chaotic preface to the coming entrance. Walking in step with the metronome, Jane and Alex emerged, clothed in black robes. Purple and gold belts cinched Jane's robe at the waist. Alex's was secured with a black belt. Their faces looked gaunt, painted with smears of black makeup. Their black-gloved hands held three-armed candelabras made of brass. Tears of black-and-white wax dripped down the spiraled candles, staining the brass. Each burned brightly, their flames glowing in Jane's and Alex's infernal eyes.

Addison turned around, searching for a way out. Two more robed cult members emerged from the direction she had begun running toward, effectively stopping her escape.

Guns were instantly drawn and pointed, Addison's at the new members, who she now realized were Veronica's parents, Yessenia and Manny. Chris's gun held steady on Jane and Tye's on Alex.

Just as the song finished, it began playing in reverse.

Yessenia and Manny pressed in closer, ushering the trio toward Jane and Alex. Toward the red *X*'s. None of the cult members wavered at gunpoint but instead remained eerily calm.

"Take your places," Jane repeated, gesturing at the *X*'s. "Time is almost up."

Addison's index finger pressed the trigger, prompting Chris and Tye to fire their weapons as well. One of the bullets clipped Yessenia in the leg. Blood soaked the bottom of her robe, but she didn't yield. Addison fired again but missed.

Tye's bullet pierced Alex in the abdomen. He remained standing in a trancelike state while the bullet seared into his viscera. Chris's bullet grazed Jane's right arm, and she too stood still despite a stream of blood trickling down her robe onto her hand. Blood dribbled from her hand to the base of the candelabra.

Manny, a tall Hispanic man with the build of a lineman, grabbed Addison, twirling her around into his arms and disarming her. He dug the gun into her temple.

"Drop your guns, or I'll shoot her," Manny demanded.

Chris dropped his gun to the ground and spat, "Let her go."

Tye hesitated at first, but when Manny pressed the gun deeper into Addison's temple, he dropped his gun in compliance. She shut her eyes tight, fighting to regulate her breathing as her heart thrashed against her chest.

"Good. Now that we are all on the same page," Jane

began, "places." Her arms glided outward like she was presenting a prize on *The Price Is Right.*

Yessenia and Manny shoved everyone toward their designated spots. Addison stood in the center of the X, Manny's gun now pointed at the back of her head.

"I figured out which character you are." Addison glared at Jane.

"What's that, honey?"

"The Wicked Witch of the West." She glared harder. If only looks could kill.

Jane laughed. "Well, funny you mention that; you'll soon see the irony. Well"—she gazed down at Addison with pity—"you won't be able to see it, actually." She retrieved a dagger that had been resting across Alex's palms. A snake twisted around the handle, its eye a purple gem. Addison had seen it before in one of Jane's glass curio cabinets.

Jane pointed to Chris with the tip of her dagger. "Hear no evil." Then to Addison. "See no evil." Last, Tye. "Speak no evil." Yessenia and Alex positioned themselves behind Chris and Tye. With brute force, the men were shoved down to their knees. When they tried to resist, they were met with violence. Alex thrust a hearty right hook to Tye's jaw. Yessenia a kick to Chris's knee.

"Oh, I'll take that." Jane pulled at the duffel bag. Addison fought back, forcing Jane to pull harder. At her refusal to let go, Manny pistol-whipped Addison in the side of the head, causing her to release the bag with a squeal. Chris lunged toward Manny in response. Alex reached around and placed a knife to his throat, chastising him.

Jane blew out the first candle, blackening her fingertips with the wick. She approached Chris and drew a triangle on his forehead with her index finger. The processes repeated with Addison, then Tye, until all three flames were extinguished.

"What's this?" Jane said, reaching for Tye's badge. "FBI."

Fear flashed through her eyes, almost too quickly to catch. Addison saw it. So she *really* didn't know who he was. He must have been telling the truth.

"This makes things interesting." Jane tossed the badge aside.

"You won't get away with this," Tye hissed.

"That's where you're wrong." Jane backed up and tapped the hourglass with the tip of her dagger. It was getting dangerously close to running out. "I've always gotten away with it, and I always will." She swayed toward Chris, running the dagger along his scalp and down to his ear. "Because my divine will always protect me." She dug the blade into the top of his ear, cutting flesh. Blood dripped into his mouth and around gritted teeth. He bit down on the pain. "And I will always honor my divine." The knife slipped deeper into the cartilage. Chris clenched his teeth harder. Short, rapid breaths pulsed from his nose.

"There is only one divine, and I can assure you it is not yours," Addison mocked.

Jane looked at Addison, sliding the blade out from

Chris's ear. "You're appalling, just like your father," she said as she brought the blade toward Addison's face. Blood from the blade smeared her cheek.

"Time's up," Jane said as she angled the blade toward Addison's right eye. Before she could stab, her arm went limp, causing the dagger to fall to the ground, where it bounced and then went still. Jane followed suit, her body jolted by a volley of bullets until she collapsed, cloaking the dagger with her robes.

Manny fell next, then Alex. Addison ran to the fountain and grabbed the duffel bag. When she turned around, she was face-to-face with Yessenia, who was positioned for attack. Addison swung the bag at her, forcing her to step back.

"On your knees," Tye demanded, wielding his gun, "you're under arrest."

Yessenia complied, interlacing her fingers behind her head. He forcefully shoved them behind her back, digging the handcuffs into her skin. A SWAT team shuffled into the courtyard. Sirens echoed in the distance as fire trucks arrived to tackle the flames that engulfed much of the factory.

Addison bolted toward Chris, almost knocking him over. Cradling his injured ear in her hand, she pressed her body into his.

"It's over now," Chris whispered. "You did it."

Local police arrived, taping off the perimeter and guiding Yessenia into custody.

Chris and Addison were loaded into an ambulance

for transport. Addison stepped aside to let the EMT take over applying pressure to Chris's ear.

"Tye," Addison yelled, just before paramedics closed the back doors. He jogged over, tucking his fallen badge back into his waistband.

"Yeah?"

"Here." Addison tossed the duffel bag over to him.

He caught it with a thankful smile.

THIRTY-TWO

ADDISON

IT TOOK twenty stitches to close up Chris's ear, which would later leave a scar. CT scans revealed no signs of internal trauma following Addison's violent pistol-whipping. She did sustain a concussion, however, and there would be extensive bruising.

Before discharge, Tye paid them a visit in the emergency room. Addison collected her discharge paperwork and moved into Chris's room, where they sat on the edge of his hospital bed.

"The evidence is amazing, so meticulous and detailed," Tye said. "From what I've seen, this is going to put away any living cult member for life at minimum. I wouldn't be surprised if Netflix comes out with a documentary once all of this is exposed."

"What about Jane?" Addison asked, though she already knew the answer.

Tye hung his head, stopping himself halfway. "She's dead. So is Manny."

"And Veronica?" Addison added.

"Already expired when authorities arrived at the scene." Tye offered a gentle touch to Addison's shoulder. "I know she was your best friend. It must be hard to process everything." He paused. "Her involvement and whatnot."

Tye backed away and leaned against the counter. "Alex is in the hospital but in custody; he'll go to prison as soon as he's released. Yessenia is already behind bars. Our team is searching for the rest of the members and have warrants for their arrest."

"How many other members were there?" Addison's curiosity kept the questions flowing.

"Amy Brighton and her husband, Connor. George Crest and his wife, Hallie. All of their kids, three in total." Tye ticked off names. "A few more that weren't part of the Oz Music Club at Berkeley that we're investigating. This is huge." He swiped his hands across the air for emphasis. "We have enough information to solve upwards of fifteen murders. The more my team digs through your father's evidence, the more we uncover."

Addison smiled, big enough to show her satisfaction but small enough to prevent pain. "I'm glad I could be a part of stopping them in some way."

"A big part," Tye said, nodding. "Your father was a good man," he added. "He worked hard to put a stop to Darkside and would be proud to know you finished what he started."

Chris rubbed her back in agreement.

THIRTY-THREE

ADDISON

CHRIS PULLED Addison in close beneath the warmth of the heater, their toes digging into the carpet. It felt good to finally be home, Addison thought. It was safe again. Surrounded by greenery, warmth, and everything that made her house a home. Neglecting the plants had pushed them to thrive. Pothos vines curled around bookshelves and trickled like waterfalls to the carpet.

As they sat curled up on the floor with a blue-and-orange crochet blanket cradling their backs, Nirvana blasted from the living room sound system. Reflecting on the previous weeks, Addison realized that her perception of her parents had shifted. The pain of abandonment had blossomed into a revelation of their love for her. They'd left to keep her safe.

After making a joint pact to quit smoking altogether, Chris dug into his pocket, pulling out a round plastic container—the kind you got from sliding quarters into a machine. He popped the pink lid off and revealed a green plastic ring in the shape of a flower.

"Addison"—he grabbed her left hand—"I don't ever want there to be any confusion about how you make me feel. From the day I met you, I knew you were the only girl I wanted to be with. I should have told you sooner, but I am telling you now. Will you marry me?"

Addison's heart pounded. Chris had remembered that she didn't want a traditional engagement ring, something she had slipped into a conversation months ago. He'd remembered green was her favorite color. Daisies her favorite flower.

"Yes," she said softly, extending her finger to receive the ring. It fit perfectly.

At the dining table, Chris and Addison set down one of the two zip drives they had stowed in their pockets at the factory.

"Should we see what's on it?" Chris asked, spinning the drive in circles on the table. They had given the other to Tye, who, after he had confirmed they were exact duplicates, had encouraged Addison to keep one.

"Yes, I'm curious what's on there." Addison stood up and went to grab her laptop from upstairs.

Back downstairs, she inserted the zip drive. A folder titled "Darkside of the Rainbow" popped up, with several smaller folders inside. The first four folders were titled "Jane," "Jack," "Alex," and "Yessenia." Each folder contained personal information, photos, and photocopies of letters written by the referenced individual. Other folders contained copies of everything else that was in the locker. Every note, every recording, every photo.

The last folder was titled "Addison," which garnered a raised eyebrow.

"Why would my name be in here?" she asked aloud as she double-clicked the folder. Inside was a single video. A still of her dad showed in the thumbnail.

When she pushed play, the video enlarged in the center of her screen. Her father didn't look like she remembered. He was an odd mix between the father she knew and her patient. He had gained weight since she'd last seen him as a kid but still had the same haircut and kind chestnut eyes. He was wearing a stained white shirt and sitting on a gray couch, likely at his house. Wherever that was. The walls were paneled in wood. Piles of junk filled the background.

"Addison"—he cleared his throat—"I hope you're finding this, though at this point I don't even know how you will. I found out where you work." His expression softened. "I am so proud of you for becoming a nurse." He straightened up, pulling his shoulders back. "I'm sure you think poorly of me; you probably think of me as the father that abandoned you. The thought of that breaks my heart every day. It has been nearly impossible to accept my decision to leave—well, your mother's and my decision. If you are seeing this video, you'll know by now about Darkside of the Rainbow. Your mother was targeted by them as a teenager, but she survived. She was young and vulnerable. In fact, her father left when she was young too, but for different reasons. She was convinced that she was chosen. At some point she was actually convinced that Darkside was good and willingly participated in their rituals, but when you were born, all of that changed for her. I'm not sure what all you remember, but we fought a lot. Our love was rough and unhealthy, but when you were born, it created a sort of soul tie between us that lasted all these years. She began drinking heavily to try to block out the reality of what Darkside was doing, what they stood for. But I wasn't on board with any of it, and Jane knew it. Jane wanted me dead. Our goal has always been to protect you, and we knew we couldn't do that if we were both dead. So I left, without a finger, and watched from afar. Collected data to one day put an end to them. It almost destroyed your mother—she couldn't find a way out—until Jane tried to kill her. She ran . . . to me. Every day we worked toward compiling all of this evidence, hoping that it would keep you, and others, safe. When Jane found out what we were doing, they tried to kill me."

He coughed, lifting his shirt to reveal a red, infected gunshot wound. "I wanted to leave you this message in case I don't ever get to tell you in person. I love you, Addison, and although you didn't see me, I have been here with you all of these years. I saw you through your punk rock phase, I watched you graduate from nursing school, and I watched you meet Chris. Creepy, I know, but I had to find out who my little girl was seeing. I have always loved you more than you'll ever know. It is my hope that Darkside gets exposed and all of their sick rituals and murders come to an end so you can go on, get married, and enjoy the rest of your life safely. Until I see you again." He finished with a nod, then reached to turn off the camera.

Addison's body shook as thick tears tumbled down her cheeks. Chris squeezed her, knowing the video was everything she needed to move forward.

———

The next morning, on the front page of every major newspaper was some variation of "1970s Cult Exposed; Dozens of Murders Linked." Although it still hurt to smile, Addison couldn't stop herself from grinning ear to ear. As breakfast sizzled on the stove and freshly brewed coffee sputtered into the pot, Addison's doorbell rang. For a moment she hesitated, then pulled the door open.

A beautiful older woman whose black hair was going gray stood on the doorstep, her eyes filled with sorrow and her smile with joy.

"Mom?" Addison said.

"There's no place like home," she replied, pulling Addison in for an embrace.

ACKNOWLEDGMENTS

I want to thank my friends and family for listening to all of my crazy ideas and reading every iteration of this book. My husband, Keith, who knows my characters just as well as I do and has been through all the ups and downs with me. My friend Corina worked hard as my trusted beta reader offering her valuable support and feedback. Finally, I want to extend thanks to my amazing editor, Eve.

ABOUT THE AUTHOR

Victoria Angelique is a registered nurse living in the Los Angeles area with her husband, Keith, and their Goldendoodle, Scoey. When she isn't working in the ICU, reading, or making up stories, she enjoys playing guitar and listening to heavy metal music.

 instagram.com/tori_angelique